LOVE CONQUERS ALL

LOVE CONQUERS ALL

AN AMISH CHRISTMAS ROMANCE

LINDA BYLER

Good Books®

New York, New York

LOVE CONQUERS ALL

Good Books books may be purchased in bulk at special discounts for sales promotion, corporate gifts, fund-raising, or educational purposes. Special editions can also be created to specifications. For details, contact the Special Sales Department, Good Books, 307 West 36th Street, 11th Floor, New York, NY 10018 or info@skyhorsepublishing.com. Good Books is an imprint of Skyhorse Publishing, Inc.®, a Delaware corporation.

Visit our website at www.goodbooks.com.

10 9 8 7 6 5 4 3 2 1

Library of Congress Cataloging-in-Publication Data

Names: Byler, Linda, author.
Title: Love conquers all : an Amish romance / Linda Byler.
Description: New York, New York : Good Books, [2022] | Summary: "Amish novelist Linda Byler spins a heartwarming tale about an Amish widow trying to survive in colonial America"-- Provided by publisher.
Identifiers: LCCN 2022021841 (print) | LCCN 2022021842 (ebook) | ISBN 9781680998313 (print) | ISBN 9781680998481 (ebook)
Subjects: LCGFT: Romance fiction.
Classification: LCC PS3602.Y53 L68 2022 (print) | LCC PS3602.Y53 (ebook) | DDC 813/.6--dc23/eng/20220505
LC record available at https://lccn.loc.gov/2022021841
LC ebook record available at https://lccn.loc.gov/2022021842

Print ISBN: 978-1-68099-831-3
eBook ISBN: 978-1-68099-848-1

Cover design by Create Design Publish LLC

Printed in the United States of America

Chapter One

THE FOREST WAS AND WHITE AND STILL. TREE branches were laden with a heavy layer of snow which had fallen during the night, the fir trees patterned with deep green needles that occasionally peeped between the mounds of snow. There was no wind, not even a gentle breeze, to disturb the pristine landscape.

From the top of the tallest elm tree, a great dark raven spread its massive wings, sending small shivers of snow through the heavy black branches. He settled back on his perch before tilting his head to one side, his curious black eyes catching sight of the lone figure struggling through the heavy snow. He lifted his head, opened his great yellow beak, and emitted a loud, unsettling shriek to announce his presence.

The figure below clutched at the knotted scarf below her chin and cast a baleful glance in the raven's general direction without breaking her stride. She hoped the call of the raven was not an omen. She had enough going against her already.

Paula was a widow, living in the unsettled region of Berks County in Pennsylvania in 1757. Her husband of eight years, Manassas Lantz, had met an early death while riding home from a twenty-mile trek for supplies. His horse had stepped into an unseen crevice, catapulting Manassas into the fearful chasm below. The search, the discovery, the funeral—all of it remained embedded in Paula's heart and mind when twilight turned into the dark of yet another unending night, in spite of two years having passed. The Northkill settlement of Old Order Amish would protect her and her two children from poverty and starvation if needed, but Paula managed to remain mostly self-sufficient.

Today, her older daughter was alone at home, watching over the wheezing younger daughter who had come down with a croup and a fever a few days ago. The normal remedies had proved seemingly useless, so when she woke screaming and coughing, Paula knew she had to take action.

* * *

Betsy was only eight years old, but that could not be helped. She had to stay with the feverish Dorcas, who was small and wan for a three-year-old child, given to strange and frequent sicknesses. Betsy had looked out for the spindly little Dorcas since the day she was born and felt deeply protective of her.

Betsy was a robust child, bright-eyed and brave. She knew exactly where the heavy piece of wood would rest on two cast iron hooks to bar the front door against invaders. She could shoot the hunting rifle if she had to, although her mother often reminded her that they were non-resistant. Betsy knew what that meant, but also knew she would do whatever she had to if little Dorcas were in danger.

Being non-resistant was about the love of Jesus. If someone smacked your cheek, you gave him the other one to smack, too. Or if a person asked for your cloak, you gave him your mantle as well. That all sounded nice, but Betsy had no intention of giving anyone anything if they came through that door.

Betsy could milk the small brown cow and carry a pail of warm sweet milk to the house without spilling a drop. She forked hay, cleaned stables, and hoed the garden alongside her mother, so her small arms and legs were well developed with healthy muscle, capable of handling duties many children her age could not.

Her skin was a nut brown, like her mother's, with black hair as straight and gleaming as hers. She had large almond-shaped eyes as dark as night, with golden lights that danced around the perimeters of her irises. Little Dorcas was pale, with a wisp of flaxen hair, the color of her father's, who was dead and buried in the new cemetery on Vesper Hill, the pine trees surrounding it bending over his grave and singing sad songs in the breeze all day and most of the night.

Betsy could hear the sound of the pine trees, a deep sighing note that struck an answering chord in her own heart. Sometimes she sat beneath the thick green fir trees, breathed in the pungent odor of pine sap, and hummed along to the cadence of this breeze as it played among the needles.

She turned as Dorcas moaned in her sleep, her dark eyes going to the bar across the door, then to the gun in the corner. She hoped God would help her mother along, but then, you never knew if He would do what you asked of Him. He certainly had not watched over her father. Her mother had repeatedly told her Dat's time was up, that it was God's will that he died, but she never really understood that way of thinking. Maybe it made sense to Mam, but it didn't keep her from crying at night. Betsy could hear her low moans of despair, the sound of her nose being blown into the handkerchief she kept under her pillow.

* * *

Paula waded on through the heavy layer of snow, glad to leave the disturbing cry of the raven behind. A chill chased itself up her spine as she thought of the raven's boisterous calls as they had wheeled above the small clearing the day of her husband's untimely demise. She shook off the thought of a second warning, a second harbinger of death. Surely no person would be required to shoulder the loss of a child so soon after the loss of a loved one like Manassas.

Manassas, her blond and blue-eyed husband, taken so soon, so abruptly. The pain had eased but still had the power to carry her into the lowest depths. This was her second winter without him, and she'd learned from the mistakes of the first, the winter she had to ask for help chopping and splitting wood and repairing wooden stakes on a leaky roof. The men had been kind, but it had hurt her pride to need their help, and already this winter she was feeling worn down with the weight of all the responsibility. Well, she'd trust God when her own strength flagged.

Her skirts were becoming heavy with moisture, her boots as if they weighed twice as much as before. She shook a fist at the raven who appeared above her, its powerful wings spread to catch the current of air only he could know. She picked up her speed, her breath coming in short heavy gasps. She held both hands over her ears and squeezed her eyes shut to rid herself of the horrible creature's mocking cry.

Oh, please God, spare me this time.

She stumbled down a gradual incline. The wagon tracks were invisible but Paula knew the trail underneath well. It was the route to her nearest neighbor, the Henry Graber home, a middle-aged couple with eight remaining children, five of them having succumbed over the years to various illnesses and infections. Malinda, Henry's wife, was well-versed in the ways of healing. To summon a doctor meant half a day on horseback, and in this snow . . .

Her thoughts accelerated with the idea of having to go for a doctor. Dorcas was so thin, so frail. She'd often wondered if it had to do with her husband's death, the days of grief and exhaustion, her milk supply dwindling to almost nothing as the poor child tossed restlessly.

She must live, she must. Her love for Dorcas was a pure, burning possession, her empty arms soothed by her skinny little form.

Betsy was so different, never needing or wanting to be held or cuddled. She had rarely rocked the independent eldest daughter—Betsy had much preferred being put to bed alone. She could see Betsy marrying young, following some adventuresome dreamer to the untamed west, never bothering to please her mother or give in to her wishes.

Her foot slipped off the side of a clump of frozen mud into a deep rut, the snow crowding underneath the heavy woolen skirt. She stumbled forward, regained her footing, and hurried on.

The Tulpehocken Creek was silent beneath the expanse of ice and snow. To the unlearned, no one would guess the creek was there, but Paula knew the water was only knee deep in summer but could turn into a rustling brown torrent in spring.

She crossed safely and began her climb up the side of Vesper's Ridge. Another mile, perhaps less. The muscles in her thighs felt the sting of weariness and she wished for a pair of snowshoes. This early November storm had caught her unaware, without sufficient firewood in the lean-to by the back door.

A beautiful flash of red caught her eye, then another. The more muted tones of the female cardinals contrasted with the deep green of the wild holly growing in profusion among the blackberry brambles.

She was rid of the sneaky raven, and the cardinals were reassuring. She didn't hear the horse at all, which did not speak well of her expertise as a woodsman or a hunter. She was shocked when a rider appeared out of nowhere, coming up behind her without warning. The hair on the back of her head prickled as she whirled and floundered before steadying herself. Wide-eyed, she gazed at the sight before her, a sweating, steaming horse, larger than most, wild-eyed, the rider drawing back steadily on the reins. The horse opened his mouth to accommodate the pressure on the tender tissue, but slid to a stop, lowering his head in obedience.

"Good day, ma'am."

Too frightened to speak, Paula stood dumbfounded.

"I'm sorry if I alarmed you unduly."

She swallowed, found her voice. "No, it's quite alright."

"May I ask where you are going? Can I assist you in any way?" The voice was deep, but with a comfortable burr. The eyes from beneath the tattered hat were curious, twinkling with good humor. A dark beard, clean-cut features, ruddy with good health, a certain masculine vitality, causing her to remember Manassas as a young groom.

She steadied herself, but kept her eyes on his.

"I'm on my way to my closest neighbor for assistance. My daughter is quite ill."

"And there was no one else who could make the journey through this deep snow?"

"No."

"Would you like to ride, and I'll lead?"

"No. Oh no. I haven't far to go."

"Then I'll walk with you."

He dismounted in one fluid motion and was standing close to her, a huge man, tall and wide and intimidating. His teeth flashed white as he asked her to lead the way. To show she retained some form of dignity, she nodded, sniffed, and set off with what she hoped would be a pace he could barely follow. She felt deeply ashamed of having felt the magnetism of his . . . well, just seeing him, she supposed. She would separate herself from any unforbidden and unwelcome longings, show him she was of the strict order of plain people who kept themselves spotless from all forms of earthly desires.

She hoped he noticed her dark shawl, the woolen headscarf covering every inch of her hair.

The sight of the log home with smoke curling from the stone chimney was the best sight she had seen all day. She felt him walking behind her, heard the creak of the leather, the snorting as the horse cleared his nostrils, but was thankful he did not make an attempt at conversation.

Stumps dotted the clearing like snow-covered sheep, each one a testimony of Henry Graber's hard work. Most of his land was converted to farmland now, with the large bank barn housing well-fed stock, the children the only hired hands he would ever need. His *gute frau* (good wife) Malinda supplied him with children around his table. A fruitful vine.

Malinda opened the front door before they arrived, her breath steaming in the cold air, her hands crossed on her large chest.

Malinda quickly wrapped her in a warm hug and Paula was horrified to feel the quick sting of unwanted tears. The annoyance of having this . . . man at her side, the guilt of her attraction, the anxiety of her sick daughter all seemed to control her emotions somehow.

"And who is your companion?"

He stepped forward, bowed gallantly, sweeping his hat off his head, loosening a tumble of thick curly hair the color of her own. Replacing his hat, he smiled at Malinda, whose own smile widened immediately.

"My name is Daniel Miller. I have just come over from the Fatherland on the *Bounty of the Seas*. I must confess, I was thoroughly lost until I met a lone figure struggling through the snow."

"Well, hello to you, Daniel Miller. I'm assuming by saying '*S'Vaterland*' you are talking about Switzerland. Schweitzaland."

"Yes, yes. My homeland in the Emme River Valley."

"Now you go put up your horse and come right on in. Paula, *komm komm.*" Immediately, Daniel told Malinda of Paula's mission. There was no time to waste with her daughter lying in *sark* (being ill). He spoke in a fluid German dialect with the endearing notes of the Swiss German in the Emme River Valley.

"Ach, Paula. Is it little Dorcas? Again?"

Turning, she commanded a boy of about ten or twelve to get Dat and the sleigh and the biggest horse. She'd prepare the medicine. Satisfied that a plan was in action, Daniel walked off through the snow to stable his horse.

Henry pulled up to the house, calling out to Malinda, who was already dressed, her satchel filled with glass bottles clutched in her gloved hand. Paula thanked her, apologized for the intrusion, but was waved off with Malinda's hearty reassurance. She was grateful indeed for the sturdy bobsled and the massive legs of the two Belgians eager to run through the snow. Paula settled herself on the seat, wrapping heavy buggy robes around her legs.

The horse's hooves were muted, a soft clopping sound, the spray of the snow whispering to her anxious senses.

Shh-shh-shh. Don't worry so, don't worry. Sh-sh-sh.

She couldn't help wondering if Daniel would stay at Malinda's house as he'd been invited to do, or whether he'd rest a bit and then continue his journey to wherever he was headed, never to be seen by her again. Daniel Miller. A nice solid name from the heart of Switzerland, her home country as well. She'd accompanied her new husband to America only ten years ago, eager for a new life and that promised freedom. Freedom to worship God in the way they felt was right, which was to dress in plain clothing, abstain from all forms of worldly entertainment and practices, to honor their own chosen ministry and live in peace and quiet with God as their judge.

As they neared her own log house, she felt another stab of anxiety. Would Betsy be alright? And Dorcas, poor suffering child. The house was small, but well built, the mountains of Berks County rising behind it like a protective father. The clearing was small, but there was enough cleared land for a garden, a small plot of corn, and a pasture—enough to meet their needs. Manassas had worked at felling trees, helping new arrivals with erecting large barns, a practiced builder of anything the community would need. They had never wanted for anything, his wages enough to provide for his wife and two daughters.

An gūta mann. She had been married to a good man.

She was off the bobsled quickly and ran to the door, trying the latch. Betsy had the bar firmly in place, so she gave a sharp rap.

"Betsy?"

"Mam?"

"Yes. Please open the door, Betsy."

Relieved to find the house fairly warm, the fire burning, and Dorcas asleep, Paula told her she had done well. Malinda came through the door, shucked her outerwear, and went to the cradle to lay a practiced hand on the child's forehead. Paula hovered anxiously, catching the crease of concern on Malinda's smooth forehead. A new wave of anxiety overtook her.

Lord, don't take my precious little one.

She felt a hand on her arm. It was Betsy, her large dark eyes filled with concern. Paula took the hand in both of her own and gave her a reassuring nod when the lump in her throat blocked the words. To break down and cry would never do. Betsy detested weakness in her mother or anyone else.

Malinda woke the sleeping Dorcas, and with measured words told Paula she was not receiving enough air in her lungs to stay awake. Dorcas managed a strangled cry before stopping to gasp for breath, her chest rising and falling sharply with the effort.

The house was filled with the sharp odor of various tinctures, and loose leaf herbs boiling on the grate in the fireplace. Malinda's broad back was bent over the struggling child as she placed warmed cloths on her chest and back and rubbed the thin white feet with the salve made of garlic and yarrow. Paula was only dimly aware of Henry coming through the front door, but gathered her senses long enough to offer him a cup of steaming tea, a loaf of sourdough bread, and the crock of molasses.

Henry returned to his home and the children, but Malinda stayed all night and into the next day. There were times they both sat on straight chairs, exhausted, sleeping with their chins on their chests, the fire burning low, cooling the log house to the point of waking them both with a chill.

At midnight, Malinda shook her head, and Paula looked at her sharply. "We can try the infused whiskey. It's too strong for one so frail, but I have no other option. Calendula and comfrey can be powerful."

"Try it, please," Paula whispered brokenly.

Little Dorcas was too weak to resist the terrible taste, so a substantial amount was ingested. The small feet were placed in very hot water, after which she was wrapped in the heaviest sheepskin blanket. When the perspiration poured from her, she emitted a weak cry, followed by a torrent of phlegm.

Toward morning, when the sky in the east showed a few pale streaks of pink, Dorcas fell into a deep sleep, the burning forehead cooled, the breathing deeper. Both women were exhausted, but the relief in the room was palpable. When Paula lit the home-made candles to dispel the gloomy interior, Malinda sighed, then chuckled.

"All you have to do, Paula, is feed me."

Paula looked up, a weary smile spreading across her face.

"Of course I will feed you. A big breakfast. Oh, so happy to do this small amount of payment."

She got down the cast iron pan, raked the coals in the fireplace, and adjusted the grate. A tablespoon, then another, of the good rendered lard from the butchering of the tremendous sow gorging itself on acorns as it ran wild in the great, thick forest. She sliced the cooked cornmeal mush congealed in a pan and set in the cold pantry, and when the lard was transparent by the heat, added slice after slice, casting an appreciative eye at Malinda's bulk. There were fried potatoes and tomato gravy to accompany the fried mush, fried sourdough bread, and molasses.

Malinda drew up her chair with the happiness showing on her whole face, saying Paula had surely made a breakfast fit for a king.

They stopped with their spoons in midair when they heard a faint "Mama."

"Oh. Oh, my Dorcas!"

Paula almost threw back her chair in order to reach her, astounded to find her sitting up in the too small cradle, blinking her blue eyes, her wispy hair twisted and matted. Paula brought her to her chest, her arms tightening as if she could never hold her close enough.

"Dorcas! How are you feeling? Oh, my dear child." Then, turning to Malinda, "I never expected her to feel strong enough in the morning to sit up and call for me. You are a miracle, Malinda."

"No no, not me."

She pointed a finger to the ceiling. "*Gott im Himmel sit gelobt und dedanked*" (God in Heaven be praised and thanked).

"Oh, indeed. Of course."

Too overwhelmed to think straight, Paula wiped away the weary tears forming unbidden.

Malinda went back to her sourdough bread and molasses, while Dorcas lay her small head on her mother's shoulder. Betsy watched from across the table, glad to see her sister feeling better but wondering whether all those tears and exclamations were necessary.

"Well," Malinda announced. "Henry said he'd be by around dinner time to see how we're faring, so I'll be here for a while yet. Do you have work for me to do? I will leave some of these tinctures and make sure Dorcas gets milk to drink. Give her some rolled oats and meat if you have it."

"Yes, there is salt pork, and venison. I was hoping to have more than one deer, but that is all I shot. The snow was early."

"Oh, indeed it was."

And so the forenoon passed swiftly as the two women chattered, drank cups of hot tea, and cuddled little Dorcas. Bathed and dressed in a clean blue dress, her hair brushed and braided into thin, flaxen strips, she was winsome child, so frail and precious.

Betsy milked the cow, fed the livestock, and swept the porch before settling down with her needlework, fretting and fussing until Paula told her to go outside with the wooden sled.

That was where Daniel Miller found her on his way to their house.

Chapter Two

WHEN SHE SAW A RIDER APPROACHING, BETSY stopped dead in her tracks and glared at him with the most ferocious look she could muster. He stopped his horse, who danced sideways, tossed his head, and chomped at the bit. Betsy watched the foam and saliva form at the corner of the horse's mouth and observed dryly, "His bit is too small."

Taken aback, Daniel gave her a level look.

"And who, may I ask, are you?"

Betsy jerked a mittened thumb in the general direction of the house.

"Betsy Lantz."

"I see. And this homestead is your family's?"

"What's left of it."

Puzzled, Daniel lowered his brows, looked toward the house and barn, then back to the child's unfriendly demeanor.

"Which means?"

She shrugged, yanked at the rope attached to the wooden sled, and told him to go ask her mother if he was that nosy. Then she strutted through the snow, easily dragging the heavy sled behind her. He watched her trek through the deep snow before urging his horse to follow her, wondering seriously whether his horse's bit was actually too small.

Henry followed in the bobsled and showed Daniel where to put up his horse, then both of them made their way to the house. They were greeted warmly by Malinda, ushered into the house, her cheeks flushed with pleasure at seeing the arrival of her husband. Paula stayed in the background, saying nothing but the usual formal greeting.

Henry exulted at Dorcas's comeback, praising his wife warmly. Again, up went Malinda's finger toward the ceiling with the same answer about thanking *Gott*.

Paula steeped the spearmint tea, her cheeks flushed with the heat from the open flames in the fireplace. Daniel sat at the table, dwarfing it and the chair on which he sat. He seemed to fill up the entire kitchen with his immense presence. Paula watched him, observed his threadbare shirt, his cuffs grayed, too short and too tight. His hair needed to be cut and he needed a shave, but she recognized the fact of his handsome face. Pleasant, good humored, without anger or guile. She had a hundred questions about him, but knew to keep everything hidden away, to appear humble, without undue curiosity.

As she listened to Henry and Daniel talk, she gleaned more information about him. He was a wanderer, born and raised in the heart of the Emme Valley in Switzerland among the strict, conservative group called the Amish, named after Jakob Ammann, the leader who broke away from the Mennonites, having had a fierce disagreement about excommunication. Daniel had grown restless under the strife that seemed to never end, coupled with the ever-burgeoning farms and leases to wealthy landowners.

He spoke in a soft, low voice, but Paula heard every word that came from his mouth. She stayed in the background, hiding the deep interest she felt.

"I don't know. There was something missing for me, something I couldn't place." The church seemed to be centered on doctrines of men, each one with his own version of Scripture, the leaders themselves in disagreement. There was a confusing mix of persecution for being an Anabaptist, and a social acceptance of certain groups, which resulted in more confusion among the brethren. Never married, he migrated to Germany, became restless, before deciding to strike out for America, where he eventually drifted to Berks County from the New England states.

Henry kept nodding his head in agreement, his wide face serious as he listened to his fellow pilgrim. Born among the Amish, it seemed to draw them into an unspoken brotherhood, an understood way of life.

"So what do you think of Berks County?" Henry asked.

Daniel smiled, revealing his white teeth and the kindness of his eyes even more.

"Oh, it's very nice country. I'm impressed with the amount of work the whole community has put into the area. The land looks good, what I've seen so far. But I was curious about this place called Lancaster County, where the soil and lay of the land are even more promising."

"Are you a farmer by nature?"

Daniel gave a short laugh. "I was. But I have rest-less feet."

Henry sat back in his chair, hooked his thumb in his wide suspenders, and shook his head.

"Not good, my friend. You need to settle down, find a good *frau* and raise a family. That will keep you from wandering."

"Do you have anyone in mind?"

"Oh yes, of course. Come to church on Sunday. There are many *schoene mait* (pretty girls) who would make you a *wunderbar gūte frau* (wonderful good wife)."

Malinda's ample body shook up and down as she laughed. She shook her forefinger at her well-mean-ing husband. "Now Henry, this man is forty if he's a day. You can't get these young girls to marry a man old enough to be their father."

Paula bowed her head and busied herself straight-ening Dorcas's skirt, clutching the thin body to hide the rush of jealousy followed by relief at Malinda's words. She seemed to be swept up by a roaring tide of emotion no Christian woman should experi-ence—certainly not one raised in the way of subdued emotion, of true humbleness of spirit and submission to God and the leaders of the church.

Daniel chuckled, his dark eyes dancing with warm lights.

"Your good *frau* speaks the truth, Henry."

Henry laughed with him then before launching into the subject of how badly the community needed a buggy maker, someone skilled in the way of producing wagon wheels.

Malinda announced the need to move on home—there was work to be done and the children were waiting by themselves. Henry was reluctant to leave the warmth of the house, saying his right hip was bothering him and what could that mean if it wasn't another storm brewing in the north?

"*Ach*, no, Henry. We just got two feet of snow, and it's only late November."

Henry grimaced as he got to his feet, looked at Paula, and asked if she had plenty of feed in the barn for her livestock and wood for the stove.

She looked up to find Daniel's eyes on hers, steady, but with a keen light bringing the unwanted rush of scattered senses. She gripped little Dorcas and took a deep breath to steady herself before answering.

"I have Betsy," she said, her smile deepening and widening. Betsy looked at Henry with no trace of friendliness.

"Betsy is my right-hand man," Paula continued. "She carries the wood to the lean-to as fast as I can split it. And the men of the church had a frolic in September if you remember."

"Yes, yes. So you're alright if another storm blows in?"

"I believe so."

"Betsy, now don't you go to the barn by yourself, if the snow and wind get heavy," Henry warned.

Betsy's dark eyes stared unblinking as she replied sharply, "I can manage. I know the trees."

"Alright, that's good, then. Paula, we'll be going now. Daniel, you're welcome to stay with us till Sunday services, if you want."

"I might be moving on. We'll see."

Paula restrained the urge to meet his eyes, to let him know the fierce resistance to the idea of him moving out of her life so quickly. She got to her feet, setting Dorcas on Betsy's small lap, and stood to wish them a safe journey home and to thank Malinda for what she had done. There was no agitation in her voice.

Daniel looked on, saw the dark-haired widow full of grace, and wondered at her bravery. She had an aura of mystery and he found himself more than a little intrigued by this tall, quiet woman.

But there was no indication of this as he shook her hand, thanked her for the tea, and moved through the door with Henry and Malinda.

Paula stood by the window, watching Henry tuck the heavy robes around his large wife, pat her shoulder, and laugh at something she said. She felt a certain wistfulness that took her off-guard. How well she remembered her own husband tucking the lap robe beneath her thigh, the heavy arm across her chest, bringing a lovely feeling of security, of love and belonging. She stepped back when Daniel mounted his horse, swinging himself into the saddle with the ease and grace of a much younger man. The horse tossed his head, playing with the restraint of the bit, his forelegs curling as he half-rose on his hind legs before dropping down, dancing on four feet.

Beside her, Betsy said, "That bit is too small."

Paula jumped, unaware she had left her seat.

"I told him so," Betsy said matter-of-factly.

"You did?"

"Yes."

"And what did he say?"

"Nothing. I think he didn't like it. But it *is* too small. His horse wouldn't do that with his mouth if he had a better-fitting bit."

"That's true, Betsy."

"You think Henry's right?"

"About what?"

"The storm."

"It could well be. Why don't we got to the barn now, make sure we're prepared if another storm blows in. Although I find it hard to believe."

"You stay here, Mam. Dorcas needs you. I'll go."

"But there might be more than you can do."

"I'll come get you if I need you."

Paula watched the sturdy child follow the path to the barn, then turned away to gather the mugs from the table. She held the one Daniel had drunk from, stroked it with her fingertips, then held it to her lips. She smiled a soft, secretive smile. Alone, away from judging eyes, from the condemnation of her conservative society, she was still a woman who had known the joys of loving a good man. Could she help her own emotion, when a man like Daniel rode into her life?

She washed his mug last, wanting to keep a bit of him as long as she possibly could, and not once did she feel shame or embarrassment.

She would pray to her Heavenly Father. He had taken Manassas, and had He now sent Daniel? Oh, it was preposterous of her to think it, but she would. She could be courageous and allow her heart a wee bit of hope and happiness.

* * *

In the barn, Betsy shucked her heavy coat and opened the gate to the box stall containing the all-purpose horse named Bob. A sturdy horse, with heavy feet and thick hair around his ankles, a heavy mane and tail, he was capable of pulling a plow through the heavy soil. Or he hitched to the buggy to travel the narrow dirt roads to the farms scattered throughout the region where services were held in the farmhouses every other Sunday, leaving a Sunday to worship at home with the children or spend the day visiting friends and relatives.

Betsy loved Bob, so she kept his stall clean and made sure he had fresh water twice a day and plenty of hay to munch on. She forked manure, carried buckets of water, cleaned out the small brown cows' feed trough, and added fresh hay. The two pigs squealed their attention, and Betsy made a face at both of them.

"No table scraps, piggies. You get only corn. You're fat enough. I hope you know your days are numbered. You'll be turned into *levva vosht* (liverwurst)."

She didn't feel the same fondness for pigs that she felt for Bob. God put pigs on the earth for people to eat, and she loved ham and sausage and bacon.

Betsy was happiest in the barn with the animals. She cared for them all without complaint. She watched out for the two barn cats who were as wild as squirrels and grew fat and sleek on a steady diet of rats and mice. They slept well in warm hollows of loose hay and scooted around the perimeters of the barn, their tails aloft like furled sails.

On her way to the house, she stopped to glance at the sky above the clearing. She noticed the blue color, the absence of clouds, the lack of wind, and remembered Dat saying if there was not a cloud in the sky, it was an omen, a harbinger of an approaching storm. They just had one, but she shrugged her shoulders and moved toward the house, going around to the back to check on the wood supply. Satisfied, she turned to memorize the placement of the trees, just in case.

Paula looked up from stirring the bean soup at the fireplace.

"Are you cold, Betsy?"

"No. The barn isn't cold when I'm working. Mam, I think Henry might be right. There's no wind, and not a cloud in the sky."

Paula straightened, looked concerned, said only, "Child!"

"I know."

"Well, there are beans and potatoes. Salt pork. We have tea and flour, enough molasses and even brown sugar. If there is a storm, we could make gingerbread cookies for Christmas."

Betsy wrinkled her nose. Dorcas looked up from her wooden blocks and clapped her thin white hands, a smile on her elfin little face.

"Cookies!"

Paula smiled at her, then laughed at Betsy.

"Betsy, you should have been born a boy. You have no indication of ever becoming a housewife."

Betsy scowled. "I don't plan on ever marrying anyone. That visitor, what's his name?"

"Daniel Miller."

"He may not know much about horse bits, but he's smart. Never marrying, just doing whatever he wants to do."

For some unknown reason, this struck fear in Paula. Was it the truth about Daniel? She spoke too quickly, too strongly, which only brought out the rebellion in her daughter.

"That is not God's will for us women, Betsy. We can never do as we want. We are created to be a help-meet to our husband, and to bear children for the Lord."

Betsy didn't snort, being raised in subjection to her mother, but she certainly had no word of agreement, either. They moved about the house in silence, the only sound the clatter of wooden blocks and Dorcas's soft voice talking to them as they fell. Paula placed three bowls on the tablecloth and three tin mugs before dishing up the fragrant bean soup.

The beans were perfectly plump, broken open along the backs, the broth rich with the backfat she had added to flavor the beans.

Steam rose from each bowl as they bowed their heads in silent prayer, thanking God for the food before them and the blessing of each other. Betsy ate hungrily, barely waiting long enough to lift her head before digging her spoon into the beans.

When the dishes were washed and put away, Paula spent the evening knitting warm socks for Dorcas, who had only one pair that wasn't darned into tatters. She felt guilty, having put off the knitting too long, a job she never relished, but was now forced to do, no matter if she enjoyed it or not. Perhaps Dorcas would have stayed well if she had warmer socks. Perhaps if she had stayed well, Paula never would have met Daniel. Floundering through the snow like that, and there he was. Imagine. She felt her cheeks flush and lifted her eyes to Betsy to make sure she hadn't noticed her thoughts. Why did she always feel judged when Betsy fixed those knowing black eyes on her?

Betsy yawned and said she was going to bed. Paula said that was fine, but the evening prayer came first. She didn't know why Betsy seemed to resist the evening prayer so much, often becoming impatient or unwilling to kneel at a chair by the table as Paula read from the German prayer book. Was it the memory of her father's deep voice as he read the passages of the book, or was it a natural inclination to resist piety? Paula knew Betsy was different, would always need a firm hand. Paula should not have to feel apologetic about announcing the evening prayer.

"Betsy," she said sharply.

Betsy said nothing.

"You are expected to come before God in prayer willingly."

"Prayer doesn't seem real. We can't see God, so why do we bother?"

Her words were like a dagger to Paula's heart. Her daughter's unbelief was a stark reminder of her single parent status. If her husband were there, he would be the one leading the family in their beliefs and religious practices. It was a job she had never asked for, never imagined she would have to do.

"Betsy, please don't say that."

"It's true."

"Perhaps in later years you will feel differently."

There was a space of silence. Then, "I hate it when you read the prayer. It should be Dat reading it, not you."

Very gently, Paula told her there was no one else to read the prayer. She added that her day felt unfinished without the calming intonation of words so familiar and so dear.

"Why?"

"I don't know, Betsy. I supposed I was raised with this prayer book. It's something my parents handed down to me, and likely their parents before them."

"Well, God doesn't always hear us or Dat would not have died in that awful way."

Betsy kicked the leg of her chair and clutched at the sides with her hands, her shoulders squared as she braced herself against her mother's words, which inevitably would fall flat, insufficient to build the slightest foundation of faith.

Paula watched and thought how much too young her daughter was to have these thoughts. She wasn't yet nine years old. But that meant there was time, plenty of time for her to have a change of heart. As she read the prayer, there was sense of pleading, of anguish in her heart. To have Manassas to lean on would be a tremendous blessing, but the reality was that she was alone. So she would lean on God's arms, the true, everlasting ones.

Paula went to bed comforted, silent prayers still cycling through her heart and mind.

* * *

The log house was nestled against the backdrop of dark, cold mountains, the bare trees huddled along its face appearing darker than the night sky. The sharp pinpoints of light, the myriad scattering of stars, began to be obliterated by a vast buildup of dark, ominous clouds laden heavily with cold air and snow. The quarter moon watched as one by one the heavens gave way to the approaching storm, and then the moon was gone, too.

Behind the dark log house the raven slept with his black head tucked beneath his powerful wing, the malevolent eyes closed in sleep. The thick spruce tree sheltered him from the worst of the storm, but he knew it was approaching. In the thicket below, the great horns of the white-tail buck lay close to the ground, the deer bedded down in the dense foliage, hidden from predators, warmed by the thick hair of his winter coat.

Down by the creek, at the base of the mountain, on the north side of the sturdy log buildings, a mink crept silently along the snow-covered bank before sliding into a secret hole beside a tree root, a still squirming deer mouse clutched in its strong jaws.

Below the ice, the clear unspoiled waters of the Tulpehocken Creek ran strong, the fish and turtles and all the amphibians hunkered down, their hearts slowed to accommodate the lessened need for sustenance, their metabolism creeping along without food.

Little Dorcas, pale and wan, lay snuggled against her mother, her breath coming in a soft, normal rhythm, the congestion and infection cleared from her chest, the cough coming only intermittently now.

Betsy woke in the dark, the only light from the stars gone now, leaving a blackened void she recognized. The storm Henry had spoken of was approaching, else why would the stars be gone?

She shivered when the high, lonesome cry of the coyote reverberated among the ridges of the mountain. Lean and hungry, the snow their greatest adversity, they lifted their noses and caught the scent of pigs, the cow, every animal in the barn at the foot of the mountain. Slowly, the leader of the pack turned to make his way to pace along the outside of the thick log walls.

Chapter Three

BEFORE DAYLIGHT, WHEN THE EAST SHYLY flirted with soft colors of dawn, there was a distant hammering closing in on Paula's senses. She dreamt of a pileated woodpecker drumming on dying sycamore, the thin, brittle bark of the tree falling like snow. Louder and louder now. Her eyes flew open and she was instantly assaulted by the rude knowledge of something banging on the front door. She lay perfectly still, the only sound the beating of her frightened heart.

When the hammering began again, she threw back the heavy layer of sheepskin blankets, chills of cold and fright running up and down her spine. The heavy plank was in place; she knew she had put it there the evening before. She reached the door, stopped, and called out, glancing at the chest of drawers with the rifle propped beside it.

"Who is it?"

At first, the answer wasn't clear, but when he repeated himself, she could not believe he had returned. With shaking fingers, she unbarred the door, drew on the latch, and opened it cautiously. She exclaimed in dismay as a whirling blast of icy air mixed with rough, hard pellets of snow blew inward, causing her to step behind the door, clutching at the neckline of her long flannel nightgown.

Daniel Miller fell through the door, his dark clothes plastered with a thick coat of the violent storm. Paula gasped, put out a hand, but stepped back as he reeled to regain his footing. When she finally found her voice, she could only say his name.

"I'm sorry," he managed finally, between gasping breaths. Paula came to her senses and moved quickly to draw the cast iron poker through the gray coals, producing a fine bed of glowing red embers. From the wood box she chose a few chunks of wood, took up the bellows, and fanned the red-hot coals. Flames leaped up, licked at the dry oak, and Daniel turned to her with gratitude. His fingers were stiff so he struggled to remove his mittens. Without thinking, Paula stepped up to help him unwind his scarf, the icy coating spraying from any removed article of clothing.

"Your floor will be a mess," he breathed as he struggled to work the hooks and eyes from his coat front.

"It's fine, don't worry. We need to get you warmed up. Why are you out in this ferocious storm?"

As she spoke, she swung the kettle onto the grate, heating water, putting on the teakettle for more. She would cook cornmeal, a fine gruel for a frozen body.

"I was thinking foolishly, I suppose. But I worried about you when I awoke and couldn't rest till I knew you were all safely at home in your house. I feared for Betsy. She's clearly a strong girl, but no child should be out in weather like this. I can tell you, if my horse was a lesser creature, I might have become lost myself. He remembered the road, never lost his footing or sense of direction. And here I am."

"Oh, don't feel unwelcome. I am humbled you thought of us at all. I thank you for that. Very much."

As she spoke, she busied herself, draping his woolen coat over a chair back, bringing another for him to remove his boots.

He held out his hands to the now roaring fire and smiled up at her as she hovered anxiously.

"And here you are, in your nightclothes, tending to this invader."

She sat opposite him, leveled her gaze, and said, "You are a most welcome invasion, believe me. I have been alone these two years, but I have had times when I was more afraid than I thought possible."

"Your husband is deceased, Henry told me."

"Yes."

"I'm sorry."

"It was the will of God."

"But His will is often hard."

"Certainly."

Paula rose, realizing her state of undress. He looked up and she found herself captive, held by the soft light in his. The fire leapt and sparked beside them and the fragrant warmth spread across the room, but neither of them noticed anything except the wonder of the lights that appeared in both sets of dark brown eyes.

Paula mumbled some senseless words about getting dressed and left the room. He stared into the fire, tried to keep his thoughts in proper perspective, and tried even harder to keep his eyes averted as she undid the heavy, black braid at the mirror by the washstand and drew a thick comb through the sheen of dark hair, coiling it into submission to the nape of her neck before setting the thick white covering on her head. She turned, a bit uneasy, to find him still staring into the fire, which proved his honorable intention.

She added salt and cornmeal to the boiling water, her slim waist bending and swaying above her gathered skirts like a flower blowing upon a breeze, her slender hands moving expertly as she stirred the mush, the smell of roasting corn permeating the house.

"What time do the girls wake up?" he asked, looking anxiously out the window at the boiling storm.

"Soon," she answered, suddenly shy.

"I can feel the strength of this storm through the log walls, I do declare," he said.

She went to the window, and he rose to stand behind her. Both could see nothing except a whirling whiteness. They listened to the howling and lamenting of the wind, like a tortured soul. Paula shivered, clasped her hands tightly to her waist. He put out a hand to place on her shoulder, but drew it back before he actually did a foolish thing like that. He caught the scent of her hair, of soap and cooking and an earthy scent that set his pulse racing.

He clasped both hands behind his back before he could think of it again.

"Soon after Manassas died, we had a storm such as this, except it was rain and wind, thunder and lightning. I have never lived through such fear. I honestly thought we would be consumed by the flashes of lightning, the roar of the thunder, as if the devil himself took glee in shaking me between his jaws. Oh, I did. I wanted to die. To join Manassas in the Promised Land. But here I am, and two years have passed."

"It can't be easy, a woman alone in the mountains."

"I don't wish to complain. Or be a burden to anyone. I'm just glad you're here. Sometimes the presence of another human being is worth more than all the gold in the world."

"Thank you."

"I don't believe you realize how much this means to me."

And then he did throw all his restraint away, lifted his hand to place it gently on her narrow shoulder, and kept it there. Both stayed very still, and there was no need for conversation.

* * *

"Mam."

The authority in Betsy's voice was sufficient to draw them both toward her, feeling strangely guilty, like children caught in the cookie jar.

"Good morning, Betsy."

She stood in her almost nine-year-old stature, a frown creasing her facial features into one of disapproval.

"Why is he here?"

"Mind your manners, please. You could say good morning, first of all." Paula's voice was clipped.

"Why is he?"

Daniel went to Betsy, pulled up a chair, sat down, and began to speak quietly. He spoke of being at

Henry's, hearing the storm during the night and being very concerned about her and Dorcas, so he rode his horse through the storm.

"That was foolish."

"Yes, it certainly was. I had no idea there could be storms like this in Pennsylvania."

"Well, now you know. So when will you go back? Now you know we're just fine."

Paula opened her mouth, said, "Betsy," but Daniel held up a hand.

"I'll go as soon as possible, and yes, of course, you'll be fine. I know you are very capable of doing chores. But it will be nice to have someone to help."

"I don't need your help."

"Alright. You can do the chores alone."

"I'm going to."

Betsy walked off to the bedroom to get dressed, then came to her mother to have her hair combed and braided. Daniel tried to keep from watching, but it was a beautiful sight, the crackling fire, the mother with her blue dress and white head covering, the child with her long black hair rippling in small waves from the tight braids, the calm silence that permeated the house while the storm raged on.

Paula met his eyes, mouthed a silent apology. He shook his head, made a waving motion with his hand.

They sat down to bowls of hot cornmeal mush, added molasses and thick, rich milk from the brown cow, and drank mugs of hot peppermint tea. Paula apologized for being out of bread, but today was baking day.

"Malinda has a rather hearty appetite, I'm afraid."

Daniel smiled widely. "She certainly appreciates good bread."

Daylight arrived slowly, the windows turning from a dark gray to a lighter hue, then the visible snow driven by the ferocious wind.

Betsy stood at the window, a crease furrowing her brow. She stepped back to look at Daniel, opened her mouth to speak, then thought better of it and closed it again. Finally, she spoke.

"I'm not sure if I carried enough water to fill the trough. How do you suppose we could do that if the storm keeps going?"

Daniel eyed her as he would a grown man.

"I'm not sure, Betsy. What do you suggest?"

She shook her head. "It will be hard to carry it from the creek."

Daniel agreed and suggested melting snow over an open fire. If they could do so on the lee side of the barn.

Betsy was eager to face the storm, so Paula brought out every heavy article of outerwear she owned, wrapped her head and face in a knitted scarf, and stood back to survey the result. She dared not laugh at all, merely pursed her lips and nodded. Daniel was bundled into his semi-dry coat, his cap and scarf, signaling the time to go.

Paula grimaced as she swung the door open. Betsy gasped and Daniel reached for her hand, which she did not pull away.

Together they stepped out into the harsh, whirling void.

Paula did her best to keep her anxiety at bay, turning to her faith as she always did, pushing back the raw memory of her beloved Manassas going over that yawning cliff. He had not been protected, but sent to a chilling death, and what would prevent Daniel and Betsy from meeting a cold frozen demise now? By His grace and mercy, all would be well.

And so she stood at the window, her face in perfect peace but her heart and mind pleading, begging God for His protection.

When Dorcas awoke, calling for her mother, she moved instantly, glad for the distraction. She sat in the armless hickory rocker, cuddling the thin form in a warm blanket, rocking and staring into the fire.

"Where's Betsy?" Dorcas croaked, before setting up coughing. Paula waited till the cough subsided before telling her she was doing chores. Dorcas was too small to realize the imminent danger, so Paula merely drew her tightly against her body and took solace from the child's trust.

She mixed the sourdough bread, washed the cups and bowls, swept the house and dusted the furniture. She tried to sing, but found the worry overwhelming and reverted to silence.

Dorcas ate a small portion of boiled cornmeal, then brought her rag doll to the heat of the fireplace. Paula could feel the cold from the log walls and added a heavy piece of good oak wood to the fire.

* * *

Daniel and Betsy found it impossible to breathe unless they held a gloved hand over their nose and mouth. Completely disoriented, Daniel allowed Betsy to go from tree to tree, cursing himself for the lack of a rope. The good fortune given them came in the fact there was a line of sturdy trees all the way to the barn, but still he was tremendously relieved to bump against the saving log wall.

Daniel needed all his strength to pull the door open, after which they fell inside, gasping, wide-eyed. Betsy's teeth were chattering, but she laughed outright and went to work immediately, calling out orders. There was enough water, but barely, so he offered to melt snow.

Betsy shook her head.

"It won't work. Why don't we just shovel the trough heaping full?"

Daniel felt like a schoolboy who had given the wrong answer. Why hadn't he thought of that before? He gave the child a sidelong glance and set to work, shoveling snow into the empty trough. The heat from the animals created enough warmth to slowly melt it.

Chickens pecked among the stalls, the rooster strutting among his many wives as he lorded it over the entire barn. He eyed Daniel with animosity, his round yellow eyes targeting him for a possible flogging if he stepped into his territory. Betsy pushed the small brown cow into position, got on her tiptoes to reach the milking stool on a hook on the post, then proceeded to fill the bucket with creamy milk while the cow chewed the good hay contentedly.

All the animals were in good shape. Even the pigs were fat and curious, putting their pink snouts against the gap in the gate, snuffling the way pigs do.

There was no undue amount of manure anywhere, and a well-used wooden wheelbarrow spoke of many cleanings.

Daniel went to the cow's stall door and leaned an elbow against the post to tell Betsy he was finished forking hay. She glared at him and told him to go away. Brown Cow did not appreciate strangers while being milked. Again, he felt chastened, and stepped away immediately.

They braced themselves for the return to the house. Daniel insisted on carrying the milk pail, though he wasn't convinced they'd have any milk left by the time they reached the house with the way the wind was blowing it and slopping the warm milk out over the edge.

They struggled from tree to tree, the atmosphere around them a sucking, angry giant showing no mercy. Daniel allowed Betsy to lead the way, reached out to catch her when she stumbled and fell, feeling redeemed from his former schoolboy status.

They stumbled up onto the porch, stamped their feet, and were rewarded by Paula drawing the door open, a glad cry on her lips, her eyes a warm beacon of welcome. She hovered and fussed, clucking at the ice on their coats, laughing at the small amount of half-frozen milk on the bottom of the bucket. Her laugh was infectious, until even Betsy's laugh rang out, followed by little Dorcas clapping her hands and spinning a few times.

"All's well that ends well, thank God," Paula said gratefully.

Daniel looked into her dark eyes and wondered how God could have led his wanderings to this woman. Had they really only met a few days ago? It seemed as if he had known her since the day he was born.

After the noon hour the storm abated. They noticed the lessening sound of the fierce wind as they lingered around the dinner table, drinking the hot apple cider spiced with cinnamon and cloves. Paula had made a venison stew thickened with potato chunks, carrots, and dried parsley, the rich fried bits of venison flavoring it deliciously. The warm bread fresh from the cast iron bake oven with churned, salted butter and apple butter was a rare treat for Daniel. He complimented her without restraint, meaning every word.

She blushed, hid her eyes, waved away the praise, saying she had been cooking for almost ten years, had always helped her mother at home.

He remembered his own home growing up. "My mother was a good cook, the way most of the women who lived in the Emme Valley were. They spent most of their days in the kitchen or washing clothes, all their time occupied by being keepers of the home. Spinning, weaving, sewing garments, darning, and patching took up any spare minute, so they were taught by their mothers, and they in turn taught their daughter. So I suppose your mother taught you well."

"My mother was never well."

Daniel raised his eyebrows.

"She . . ."

Paula hesitated. Should she honestly tell this man about her escape from a home holding many secrets? Would he think less of her? Why should she convey the past with its darkness and fear?

She met his eyes, shrugged.

"I'd rather not talk about it just now."

Betsy, never one to miss a thing, asked her mother why not.

To which Paula had no answer. She changed the subject immediately.

"Seeing that the storm continues and Daniel cannot leave, why don't we bake? Christmas is not too far away and my supplies have been replenished by the elders of the church, so why not?"

Daniel laughed. "I am not good in the kitchen. Never helped my mother with anything. There was no need, with a gaggle of sisters."

"Oh, we'll put you to work, don't worry." Paula smiled.

There was a flurry of activity after the dishes were washed and put away, the wooden bowls on the table soon filled with the rich smell of ginger, molasses, cloves, and other spices. Paula measured and stirred, finishing the cookie dough with her hands to incorporate the flour better.

Daniel put logs on the fire to heat the bake oven built into the chimney, then swept the hearth with the small willow broom, glancing over his shoulder to see if Paula noticed.

She hadn't, but Betsy pointed a finger, said, "Look, Mom. Daniel is sweeping the hearth, the way Dat used to do."

Paula stopped mixing and watched Daniel finish sweeping the sawdust into the fire, her face softened.

"So he is."

There was no emotion in her voice, only a level observation of Daniel's careful sweeping. Betsy climbed a small stool to get down the metal cookie cutters, unaware of having spoken about anything unnecessary, and Paula said nothing more for some time. The coziness of the house filled with the scent of spices and sugar, the warmth of the fireplace, and this man keeping her from being alone in the mountains in such a storm all felt like a gift, something received with great thanksgiving. Betsy's words had thrust her into the past. Remembering Manassas made her feel a bit guilty, as if she had already become a merry widow, forgetting the sadness, the silent grief that had been her constant unwanted companion for so long.

And she felt disloyal to him, to her first husband, he of the guileless heart, the one who had borne her safely away from the wretchedness of her mother's condition.

Daniel felt a sudden change in the atmosphere and asked her if he'd done anything wrong.

"No, no. Of course not," Paula assured him hurriedly, turning her back to retrieve the rolling pin. But there was something amiss, he was sure of it. He decided to let it go, not wanting to take away the cookie baking experience from the girls.

He watched Paula roll up her sleeves, careful to keep the elbows covered, before grasping a section of the stiff dough and placing it on the floured dough board, her strong forearms contracting as she plied the rolling pin to create a thin layer of perfect dough.

Betsy bit down on her tongue, her eyes intent on creating a perfect cutout, as Paula leaned over to watch. Together, they formed eight gingerbread men, added walnut pieces for eyes, and a string of smaller ones for a wide smile.

"We need raisins and frosting," Betsy said.

"Neither one is available, I'm afraid," Paula said.

"They'll be delicious without," Daniel added. "It's been a long time since I had a gingerbread cookie. I'm sure they'll be delicious."

Betsy eyed him with the same disconcerting look as the day they'd first met, standing in the snow, rigid with disapproval.

"Why didn't you have any cookies?" she asked in a clipped tone.

"Riding from one place to another without having a home, I'm not sure where I would have baked cookies," he said, laughing as his mouth turned down even farther.

"I don't know why you're here. You could be a robber, or maybe you plan to hurt us."

Paula was aghast.

"Betsy."

"Well, we don't know."

Daniel held up a hand. "You're right, Betsy. I could be. But the nice part is, I'm not. I lived a perfectly normal life, except for wandering from place to place, never settling down long enough to have a permanent home."

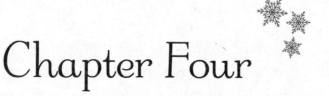

Chapter Four

THE FIRST TRAY OF COOKIES WERE PERFECT—plump, dark brown, and glistening. Paula's cheeks were flushed as she lifted them carefully onto a checked tablecloth, smiling as the girls squealed their joy. Between her thumb and forefinger, Paula held a pinch of white sugar, slowly sprinkling it into place to form a sweet dusting on each cookie, using it as sparingly as possible.

Daniel felt as if he had landed in the middle of some place close to paradise as Paula handed him a plate of cookies and a warm mug of tea laced with honey. Her hair, parted in the middle and combed into two sleek, black wings, made him wonder if the angels all parted their hair in such a fashion. He imagined running the tips of his fingers across the shining surface. No other woman had ever made him think such strange thoughts.

And still he was at ease, comfortable, as if he had every right to feel this way. He drank the perfectly flavored tea and ate three gingerbread men in quick succession before realizing the light through the window was changing.

A quick stab of regret coursed through him. The end of the storm meant it was inappropriate for him to be at the widow Paula's house. He got up from his chair and walked to the window, saw the lessening snow, the calming of the wind. As he watched, a lavender hue to the west deepened and spread until the storm clouds appeared to have a tear in them, like fine cloth cut by a sharp knife.

He said nothing, thinking perhaps there might be another storm brewing on the heels of this one. Paula watched as he stood at the window, the top of his head only a few inches from the ceiling, his wide form filling the entire window. She, too, thought of the storm blowing itself out and was filled with the same numbing sense of disappointment.

She kept baking cookies, laughing with the girls as they decided it was better to bite off the whole head first, little Dorcas giggling and reeling across the room. The fire burned brightly and the candles flickered on the table as Paula moved from table to oven and back again.

They didn't need much supper after all the cookies, so they enjoyed the warmth of the room, the calming silence of the storm now having blown itself out.

Daniel sighed contentedly.

"This is almost too nice. A man could easily get used to this."

Dorcas looked up from the floor where she was feeding bits of cookie to her rag doll. "You can live here," she said, her high lisping voice barely discernible.

"Did you hear her, Paula?"

"What?" She turned from the heat of the bake oven, her eyes going to his. He had said her name, making it sound different, somehow.

"Dorcas said I can live here."

"Dorcas, now why would you say such a thing?"

"I like him," she said sweetly.

Betsy frowned, not liking where this was going at all.

"Mam would never let you live here, because you'd have to get married, and she told me she would never do that."

She met Daniel's eyes, claiming complete victory. *He may as well not even think about it,* her eyes said. *She's mine.* He glanced at Paula to see if she would deny it, but her back was turned—perhaps she was pretending not to have heard.

For the next few hours he was aware of a creeping weariness but blamed the hard work of getting through to the barn. *What a young upstart,* he thought of Betsy. No doubt he had been impressed by the girl's strength and bravery, but she needed a firm hand or she'd wind up growing into a rebellious young woman. He tried not to take her clear dislike of him personally—of course she was still missing her father.

The whole world, as far as he could see, was covered in an unbelievably heavy layer of snow. As twilight fell, the western sky was a palette of pinks, oranges, and reds with the distant roar of an approaching wind bending the tops of the trees, sending great white swaths of snow into the air. He realized the aftermath of the storm could easily keep him from traveling for days if the wind was as fierce as it sounded from a distance.

He wanted to stay for the night. He wanted to stay for the next day and another night. A week. A month.

For the first time in his life the thought of swinging a leg over the saddle and riding off through the storm was depressing. He had no heart for it, this constant seeking of what he might find on the opposite side of the mountain. He had ridden across dozens of them, found hundreds of creeks and valleys and too many rivers to count. Pennsylvania was beautiful country, but what would be beyond the next boundary? And the next?

He didn't know.

He watched Paula arrange the cookies into a metal box lined with a linen cloth, then place the lid on top before storing it in the tall wooden cupboard by the back door. She told the girls it was bedtime, then helped them into their flannel nightgowns, drawing warm socks over Dorcas's feet.

She looked at Daniel. "Would you like to read the *Abend Gebet* (evening prayer)?"

"I will, certainly. It would be an honor."

She handed him the small black book, almost painfully shy, then turned to kneel at a chair with the girls. He knelt at the same time, found the well-worn page, and began to read the familiar words.

"*Unser Vater in dem Himmel*" (Our Father who art in Heaven) . . .

Paula's heart raced at the sound of his deep baritone pronouncing the beloved German words. Indeed, the man was no imposter. The mark of a true Amish man was the ability to read German well, and he could certainly do this. When the last "amen" was pronounced, she could not meet his eyes but busied herself getting the children to bed. A sense of urgency seemed to make the task of getting them tucked in longer than usual, as if he might be gone when she returned.

But he was there, sitting in a chair, drumming his fingertips on the tabletop, agitated. She moved quietly, placed the kettle over the fire.

"Tea?" she asked.

He looked up. "Yes."

The clock on the wall ticked loudly, the pendulum marching along the passing of time, too quickly. Much too quickly. He realized the futility of this evening with Paula, without the courage to speak his mind. Quickly, he prayed an unfamiliar prayer—the prayer for courage to cross this final mountain.

"Looks like the storm is over," he remarked, which was not at all what he wanted to say.

"The wind is getting up, though."

"Yes."

Hurriedly, she got up to fill the cups with tea and checked the level of water in the kettle.

"I'll have to leave as soon as the weather permits it. If the elders of the church knew I was here, they would never allow it."

Paula looked up sharply. "They don't know."

Silence hung between them for a long moment.

"I'm curious about the remark you made about your mother," he said, finally, partly because he really was curious and partly because he didn't yet have the courage to tell her what was really on his heart.

She waved a hand. "Some things are best not spoken of."

"Tell me."

"Why should I? You are a stranger."

"Am I? Paula, am I really?"

Quickly, she got up, moved the kettle, reached for the long cast iron poker, and began to stir up the fire. When she turned, he asked her the same question, without expecting an answer.

She became agitated then, her hands fluttering to her throat as if to still the light pulse beating there. She opened her mouth to speak, her face pale and uneasy.

"Yes. Yes, you are a stranger. And if you know what is good for you, you will ride away from here as soon as possible."

"Paula."

"Don't. Don't say my name. You don't know me. You have no idea who I am. Ravens follow me and call out their bad omen to me. Didn't you wonder why I only have two daughters, and none for almost six years? Why my husband died? Didn't you wonder why I have an unusual name?"

Her voice was barely above a whisper, hoarse, tormented. He left his chair and went to her, but the fluttering hands left her throat and were held in front of her, palms out, as if to form a wall.

"Don't. Don't come near me."

"I only want to know why you are talking in this manner. What do you mean by ravens? And no, I hadn't given a thought to you only having two girls."

He could see the inner struggle as she fought the desire to tell him what was on her mind versus the need to cast it aside as meaningless. He took her hand and led her to a chair, filled the mugs with the hot tea, and sat down across from her.

"Tell me everything. We are safe here tonight from prying eyes, so we can tell each other what we feel."

"I am never safe."

"Paula. We are all safe in Christ, you know that."

"I was born under a curse."

Shocked, Daniel was speechless, but his eyes never left her face. Paula paused for a moment and then her words came quickly, as if a dam had been opened and they were flooding out.

"I was meant to be a boy. My mother could never accept me, so she named me Paula. For Paul. She said I was born under the sign of the waxing moon, meaning the time of thistles and pestilence. She put up a hex sign on our barn to protect the family from the evil spirits that lurked in the far corners of our fields. She burned incense, read her Bible, and beat me regularly, to cast out the demons, she said. That was why I came so willingly to America with my new husband. To get away from her. I have found a measure of peace, and a fledgling faith, but I am never free of my mother's eyes. She is with me always. I hear her voice—the ravens know it, and follow me, bringing bad luck. Manassas died. He died. And now, almost, Dorcas followed him. My mother told me I would see sorrow to the end of my days. Malinda, bless her, says none of these things are true, it is all fueled by superstition, and that my mother does not have a healthy mind. She could be sick, although I have never heard of such a thing."

She paused, watched Daniel's expression with agonized eyes.

Daniel's eyes softened, liquefied until the tears dropped from his lashes. He got up from his chair, unfolded to his great height, and took her hand so tenderly she looked afraid.

"Come."

She went hesitantly, but when he took her into his great arms, she stayed gladly, laying her head against the width of his chest and closing her eyes.

"Do you feel my heart beating?" he asked, soft and low.

She could not speak for the desperation of her crying, subdued, hushed, her chest heaving.

"Paula, as sure as my heart is beating, God loves you. He is much more powerful than any imagined bad luck or evil spirits. Your mother's words are rubbish. Paula!"

Shocked to feel the agony of her sobs, he held her even closer, and she shrank against him to hide in the solid safety of his strong arms. He had never held a woman in his arms, had never kissed anyone, but was gripped by the need to convey his caring, to comfort her, to make everything right. She lifted her face awash in tears, tried to say what was on her mind, but found herself too deeply in despair.

He loosened his arms, found his rumpled handkerchief, and applied it tenderly. She reached up to cover his hand with her own, to swipe at the unwanted tears. They both began to talk in broken, confused sentences, until she got on her tiptoes, placed the palms of her hands on each side of his face and found his lips with her own. For the space of time it took his heart to continue beating, he thought perhaps he had died quickly and gone to paradise. But the woman he held was Paula, here on Earth, and if this was what it meant to kiss her, well then, here was where he'd stay.

He would never give this up, not to the end of his days.

After a while, she moved away, smoothed her apron, and dried her face. She placed the tips of two fingertips on her mouth, looked deeply into his eyes, and said very calmly, "I can't believe I did that."

He laughed, then felt like weeping, before he laughed again.

"Paula."

It was all he could manage. Her name would be on his lips forever. She was his. He couldn't tell her just yet, but she was.

"You'll think me wanton."

"No. You could never be anything awful or bad or evil."

"You don't believe my mother's words?"

"No. Never."

"But for all my years on earth, I have believed them. I know I still do. I honestly believe people can be born under a bad sign."

"I can't persuade you, Paula. Only God can help you out of the grip of something so wrong."

"But you have to understand. The raven followed me all the way to Malinda's house. He lifted his wings and shrieked at me. He follows me. I tell myself and the girls it was God's will for Manassas to die, but in my heart I believe it was the beginning of sorrow and there are many more to come."

"You met me on the way to Malinda's house."

Only for an instant, she allowed her eyes to contain the ray of joy at his words, but then she shook her head.

"How can I know you won't be the next sorrow?" Suddenly, she swung a hand. "Oh, go, just go. Ride away from me. Don't let me see you ever again. Three babies. I lost three of them. Two little boys and a girl. They left me long before it was time."

She became quite fierce, then, so that he felt almost afraid of her. "You want to join the babies and Manassas?"

He shook his head. "No. And I have no reason to believe I will."

She sat down, her head bent, her neck in a graceful arc. A soft moan escaped her pale lips.

"I wish to be free of this curse."

"You are free, Paula."

There was no answer. The wind battered the windowpanes, shrieked around the log joints, and whistled down off the mountain, driving great white curtains of snow to form exquisite drifts. They both sat listening, he with a grateful heart to be held captive in the warm house with Paula, she with a myriad of emotions she could never unravel. Like a knotted, tangled skein of yarn, there was no beginning and no end to the threats of her demented mother. Not even the width of the Atlantic Ocean could put enough space between her harsh words and the length of willow switch raining on her shoulders.

As she sat in agonized remembering, he sat opposite her at the wooden table, resolve strengthening every living breath. He would help her through this, somehow, sometime. He would never leave this community, and with that thought came a certainty, a complete knowledge of God's will. It no longer mattered if the storm blew itself out; he would never ride away.

He felt lighthearted, eager to start his new life. So he swung the subject from darkness to light, telling Paula he'd likely stick around for Christmas. Would she like a ride in Henry's little cutter?

And Paula smiled, touched his arm, and said she would be pleased to have a ride if there was room for Betsy and Dorcas.

They talked on until past midnight, the subject often swinging back to her tortured childhood, back to the place kept in her mind like a painful, festering sore.

She placed herself firmly in his arms and kissed him good night—the sweetest, most endearing thing he had ever experienced.

She was a miracle, an angel, even if she was a troubled one.

* * *

Morning dawned, pale and cold, the wind finally having blown itself out. When the sun rose over the mountain to the east, the forest and surrounding clearing was dazzling white, untouched by anything or anyone. The drifts were like beautiful sculptures, the overhangs from banks and cliffs crafted beyond human skill, the edges as delicate as lace.

Daniel was out shoveling pathways at the crack of dawn, the shovel like a toy in his large hands. Paula watched from her station at the window, thinking how long she and Betsy would have to work to clear half of the snow he did in so short a time. She felt grateful but would not allow herself the pleasure of thinking this would be a lasting blessing.

He would ride off to some unknown destination, forgetting he'd even spent a few days with them. He'd forget the talks and . . . She felt the heat creeping into her cheeks, felt ashamed and weak. It was best he keep going, best for him and for her. She could manage very well on her own. She'd done it for two years, or almost, and could do it again.

When Betsy woke up, the way to the barn had been cleared, the animals fed and watered, the cow milked. Betsy blinked the sleep from her eyes and asked if Brown Cow had allowed it.

Daniel looked at her, at the wise black eyes evaluating him as if she already knew the answer and was waiting to see if he had the courage to tell her. Which he did, of course, with a great laugh, the good humor crinkling the outer corners of his eyes.

"She didn't like me at all, Betsy. She sidestepped and kicked until I put hobbles on her, but she still didn't like me milking her."

"I figured. She likes me."

She smiled her small, pinched smile, as if her pride would not allow her a wider, more genuine one. Daniel caught her eye, though, and sent another great laugh through the house, and she almost laughed with him, but not quite.

Paula smiled, her cheeks flushed.

"But he did get a nice amount of milk, Betsy. We can have rolled oats and molasses and milk for breakfast. Too bad the chickens aren't laying. The days are too short this time of year."

The fire in the fireplace crackled and burned, flames leaping high as more logs were piled on, warming the small house as well as possible. The corners were always cold, but no one seemed to mind, being used to a fireplace as the only source of heat.

Breakfast was delicious, with the salt pork and fried bread with butter, the rolled oats creamy with the rich warm milk. They lingered over mugs of tea, joked with the girls, but had hidden messages that were only for each other. Paula wrestled inwardly with all of it, alternately enjoying the moments together, deciding it would be best if he left, and wishing she hadn't shared her story and let him see her fear and bitterness.

"Well, I'll be off, then," he remarked.

"Will you come back someday?" Betsy asked.

"We'll see which way the wind blows."

She frowned. "What does that have to do with it?"

"It's just an expression."

Perplexed, she fixed him with that cold stare.

"You'd better do something with that bit. Your horse's mouth is not comfortable."

"Betsy," Paula said, ashamed of her daughter's forthrightness.

"She's probably right. Do you have a general store or a harness maker here in the community?"

"Yes. Tobias Stoltzfoos. Over on Asper's creek. It's probably a good ten or eleven miles. I wouldn't imagine you would want to ride that far in this snow."

Paula's eyes never left his face as she spoke, and neither did his. Looking deep into her eyes, his message was clear, even if they spoke of mundane things. He cared very deeply about her, did not want her to forget him, felt sad to be going away. But the conservative way of the Amish would never allow him to stay any longer, both knew well. What had occurred behind closed doors would be scandalous, no matter whose ears it reached, but both felt secure, the secrecy carefully guarded.

Paula clasped her hands behind her back so as not to risk reaching out to touch him, but she allowed her eyes to convey the strong feelings of sadness and regret at his leaving. Betsy and Dorcas waved goodbye as he let himself out the door, then hurried to the window to watch as he walked to the barn. When he reappeared, his horse was rearing up on his hind legs, shaking his head, sidestepping and prancing as he struggled to control him. When he finally settled down, he rode off down the narrow strip he hoped was the dirt road he'd ridden in on, then allowed the horse to have free rein. He felt the power beneath him as he surged forward, sending the snow flying high on either side.

From the tree behind the barn, where the pasture fence dipped to the now silent creek, the sleek black raven lifted its wings and let out the loudest raucous cry it ever had.

Chapter Five

Unseasonably warm weather followed the two storms, turning the countryside into a soggy, melting quagmire. Creeks pushed the thin ice along their banks like broken dishes, followed by raging torrents of muddy water that picked them up and hurled them along to fling them around bends where the water overflowed its banks, leaving the broken ice particles to melt in the sun.

Roads were impassable, with excess moisture beneath the heavy layer of snow turning them into slippery, slushy, water-clogged pathways.

Doing chores proved to be an annoying endeavor, with wet snow and torrents of icy runoff seeping over the tops of boots, soaking through leather as if it were only thin fabric. The barnyard was like a pond, with Brown Cow slogging through the snow, her sharp cloven hooves turning the dirt beneath into a runny brown mash.

November came to an end, with no one on the small homestead except Paula and the two girls. Travel was an impossibility, so she could not hitch up the faithful all-purpose horse and attend church services, for which she felt a deep regret. To be among friends and loved ones every other Sunday meant so much—the sermons and singing, kneeling in prayer with those she loved, was a huge amount of courage served up to sustain her from week to week.

She did not allow herself to dwell on the memory of Daniel. She feared for his safety, riding across a countryside saturated with snow runoff, the rivers and creeks swollen to five times their normal size. She trusted he was well-versed in the ways of the land, and let it go, or tried to. At night, when the house was dark and still, she could picture his face, the width of his back, his large hands, and was engulfed in a mixture of longing and sorrow. Grief for what might have been. She'd frightened him away with her maudlin crying, her dreadful account of her mother's heresy. Perhaps it had been her own fault, through the bare fact she was born a girl when her mother wanted a son to please her father, who was no less harsh and formidable.

Paula sighed as she sat at the window, catching the rays of the warm yellow sun, her fingers moving in a blurring rhythm, the knitting needles flashing in the light, creating a pair of socks for Dorcas. A blue pair, with a line of yellow along the top. Too fancy, but the color would be hidden by her long, pleated skirt. She would be so happy to receive a new pair of socks, especially a blue pair with a yellow line across the top. Paula smiled to herself, thinking of Christmas and the new rag doll she planned on making. Dorcas would never part with the old, tattered one named Lizzie, so she would tell her it was a new sister. If the weather turned more hospitable, she would try very hard to get to the general store in the town of Morris. There she would purchase a stick of peppermint for each child, and perhaps a new slate and chalk for Betsy to prepare for when she would begin to attend school. If her coins held out, she would consider fabric for a new Sunday dress, then allow Betsy to wear the Sunday dress she had now to school. She believed the three tucks she had sewed along the hem would be sufficient to lower the skirt to a proper length, so it would be serviceable, indeed.

"Mam?"

It was Betsy from her place at the wooden table, where she was piecing patches of loose homespun fabric, her brow knitted in concentration.

"Yes, Betsy?"

"If you knew how much I hated this you would never make me do it."

"Do what?"

"Sew these patches. I can't sew a straight line."

Paula sighed, put her knitting aside, and went to examine the work. The stitches were much too long, would never hold the pieces together, but Paula did not say this. She merely smiled and said she would learn with more practice. She encouraged her to try making smaller stiches, which did nothing for Betsy's dark mood.

"I can't."

"Oh, I think you can."

"I don't know why I couldn't have been born a boy. I like to do chores and work with the animals and chop wood and carry it and stack it. Why do I have to learn this?"

She flung the misshapen patch across the table where it clung to the edge before slipping to the floor. Dorcas looked up from her play, put down the rag doll, and bent to pick it up.

"Here, Betsy," she said sweetly.

Betsy glowered at her and snatched it out of her hand before flinging it across the table again. Paula reached down to grasp her arm firmly and told her that behavior was unacceptable.

"Enough, Betsy," she said sharply.

Betsy sat on a chair with her face to the corner to round out her time of discipline, with Paula keeping watch as she kicked the rungs of the chair, slid sideways until she barely hung on to the seat, or coughed continuously and unnecessarily. Finally Paula sent her to don her coat and scarf to go out to the barn.

At times like this, she keenly felt the need of her husband, the faithful Manassas, a good disciplinarian, a loving father. She pushed back the urge to feel sorry for herself for the hundredth time, knowing this was a trap from Satan, a quicksand consuming her entirely, the times she could find no reason to hope or trust in God's mysterious way.

* * *

As the week went by a cold wind blew in from the north and the temperature dropped to an alarming single digit, freezing every wet lowland and pile of slushy snow as hard as a rock. The freeze meant she could hand wash the white coverings, sponge clean and iron her gray Sunday dress, and prepare to attend services, which she could only guess would be at Ezra Garber's, a distance of less than five miles. She spent all day Saturday humming the slow German "lieda," her heart lifted to think of greeting the numbers of the community with a holy kiss, a warm handshake, and words of gladness. She was starved for female companionship, for snippets of forbidden gossip and giggles of genuine humor.

She cleaned the small log house from one end to the other, scrubbed the oak floors with a brush and hot lye-soaped water, crawling back and forth on her hands and knees, shooing Dorcas out of the way as she went. She washed clothes and bedsheets and tablecloths and hung them on the rope leading to the sturdy maple in the backyard, her fingers numb with the cold. The water steamed up into the cold air as she swiped the laundry stick into the depth of the galvanized tub, fishing out articles of clothing she wrung out by hand, squeezing and twisting with all her strength before depositing them into the woven basket made of reeds from the creekbank. She loved the chore of washing clothes, the cold air in the lean-to mixing with the boiling hot water, the dazzling whites of bedsheets and tablecloths.

After Manassas died, this was her place to weep all the heavy sorrow filling her tormented heart, allowing the endless tears to mix with the soapy water. It was healing, somehow, the tears, the evidence of her humanity here on earth mingling with the bedsheets where he had lain. He had loved her, had lain with her on these sheets, and this was enormously comforting.

She dusted the furniture, washed the wooden chairs and table. She put extra lye soap in a steaming bucket of water and scrubbed the hearth till her face felt on fire, the glowing red embers giving off the necessary heat. She baked the loaves of good sourdough bread, wrapped them in oilcloth, and stored them on the pantry shelves.

Then she heated water for their Saturday night bath behind the heavy curtain strung on a rope beside the fireplace. She was alarmed at the poor thin body of her younger daughter, pale and shivering, ribs like the teeth of a comb. Her thin blond hair seemed almost translucent, so pale and sparse. A moment's anxiety swept over her, forcing her to pray, asking God to give her strength, to keep her from harm.

I can't live without the comfort of Dorcas, she thought, yet again. Betsy would not allow her mother to help her with anything—no back scrubbing, and certainly no hair washing, which was only done once a month. Paula figured if Betsy wanted to walk around with dried soap in her hair, well, then, she could. Betsy had nut brown skin and round, muscular limbs, well-formed shoulders and an appetite to match. Countless times in the past month she had become thoroughly soaked in the snow, which only increased her appetite, put brilliant color in her cheeks, and gave a spark to her eyes. Those were the suppers she would eat three slices of bread with molasses and half the bean soup.

* * *

Sunday morning Paula rose before dawn, took down the lantern, and made her way to the barn. Bob nickered a warm greeting, so she quickly gave him a measure of oats to keep him occupied while she brushed his heavy coat, raking out the tangles in his mane and tail before throwing the heavy leather harness across his back. She fastened every snap and buckle, then clapped a hand affectionately on the soft part of his neck.

"Good Bob. *Schöena gaul*" (Nice horse).

She fed the pigs and chickens but did not milk Brown Cow. She was drying up, so milking could wait until the evening.

She shook the girls awake, then wet their hair and rolled it tightly along their foreheads, pinning it to a coil on the backs of their heads. She helped them in dress in blue Sunday dresses, white pinafore-style aprons, white head coverings, and heavy black shoes and stockings. They ate a thin gruel of cornmeal mush with molasses and milk, banked the fire, then dressed in heavy coats, black woolen shawls, and black headscarves and bonnets. There was no time to think about Dorcas crying and shivering in the cold buggy parked beside the barn; she needed Betsy to hold the shafts high to back Bob into them, something he tended to resist.

After a few frustrating tries, he was hitched to the buggy. She kept the reins in her hands as she climbed in after Betsy, and then they were off, the steel rims on the wooden buggy wheels shrieking against the frozen snow, which sent shivers up Paula's back.

They bounced over frozen ruts, tilted narrowly through mounds of frozen slush. Paula held her breath going across the ice on the narrow creek, but they made their way safely across.

Betsy exaggerated being tossed from side-to-side until Paula told her sternly to stop that, this was the Sabbath. Whether she took the admonition to heart was anyone's guess, Paula thought ruefully.

The road to the church services was even more hazardous than Paula had feared, the buggy creaking in protest as it slid up embankments, sank into slippery ruts before righting itself, only to be thrown sideways around the next turn. Bob plodded steadily on, taking his time, surefooted as a small burro, never wavering in doing what was required of him. But she felt great relief when she saw another buggy ahead of her turning into the homestead. She guided Bob to the right, past dense fir trees with a growth of thick thorny branches growing unkempt across the frozen mud of the lane leading to the buildings.

Ezra Garber was not known for his farming ability, or for almost anything else, except successfully siring and raising the astounding number of ten boys and six girls, each one tall and reed thin with identical brown hair, brown eyes, and varying degrees of protruding teeth. The oldest son had married at the age of nineteen, followed by a brother who ran off to Tennessee the following year, leaving a grand total of fourteen, the youngest being a few months old. His wife, Verna, was an amiable soul who lived a carefree life cuddling babies and cooking. Ezra made up what he lacked in ambition by being a good father, so when the Garber supplies ran low, the brethren were always happy to chip in and help them out.

Loose shingles slapped in the morning breeze and Paula knew the snow cover was a blessing the way it covered a yard littered with various objects and unkempt weeds and bushes. The house was made of logs and was larger than some to accommodate the burgeoning family. When services were there, the benches were set in a large room, which was better to hear the sermon; in many homes, the women were in a separate, smaller room, away from the minister.

Ezra greeted her warmly, shaking her gloved hand, then bending to the girls.

"I'll get Bob," he said. "You just go on in."

Paula thanked him before straightening her shawl, brushing the horse off the front, and pulling off her heavy gloves as she walked to the house.

She was early, so there were only two women standing in the main room, besides Verna and a half dozen children of various heights.

"Oh, Paula! I wondered if you'd dare to venture out. So good to see you. *Komm*, Dorcas. Let me get

your shawl and bonnet. *Hesslich*. Are you cold?"
Dorcas shook her head shyly.

Betsy busied herself untying her own bonnet, eyeing Verna with distrust. Dorcas gazed into Verna's
face, her pale skin almost blue against the black of her
shawl, and Paula felt the familiar wrenching worry.

She shook hands, kissed each woman with the
holy kiss of greeting, then leaned close to Katie
Weaver and whispered, "How are you?"

Katie's eyes shone with the glad recognition of
good friends who have been apart too long, and said
softly, "Oh, keeping the house warm and the children fed."

They laughed softly, their hands to their mouths
to appear circumspect. The Sabbath was a time to be
sober, a time to contemplate on the seriousness of the
Christian walk. So they stood quietly, saving more
conversation for the afternoon. Women and children
began to fill the house, bringing in the earthy scent of
the outdoors, the cold air and odor of heavy woolen
outerwear that was only ever spot cleaned. Soft mur-
muring moved up and down the line of women;

babies peeped out over tightly buttoned cloth shawls until their mothers unbuttoned them.

When the ministers filed in, shaking hands and commanding an air of great respect, the women paid attention, adjusting their wide covering strings and hoping for approval of those in authority. Dress was a serious matter and those who stretched the limits for the sake of *hochmut* (pride) would be paid a visit by the deacon and an accompanying minister. Paula felt a stab of guilt as the kind bishop's gaze rested on her face, so she kept her eyes lowered respectfully. To have a man in her house, a stranger, for the length of time Daniel had been there was never remotely permissible, of this she was fully aware. She could only hope no one would find out.

She filed in with the rest of the women, going according to age, their children on their laps or filling the gaps between them. The single girls filed in, followed by a blast of frigid air as the single men followed soon after.

As was her habit, Paula kept her eyes lowered respectfully, not wanting to be one who examined every youthful man, measuring the length of his hair according to the *ordnung* (laws) of the church. Later in the day, these busybodies might approach a mother whose son was *ungehorsam* (disobedient) and admonish her roundly, telling herself the rebuke was done in Christian love. Really it was pride, intolerance, impatience hid well under the deceptive cloak of piety, which accomplished nothing except sending the poor mother home with a heavy sense of failure.

Paula had witnessed this on occasion and had always felt the disgust rising in her, only to turn away and let it go. With what measure ye mete, it shall be measured to you again. Life could be tricky after you chose to follow Christ. And here she was, more *ungehorsam* than anyone, having allowed Daniel to stay in her home for two nights.

She looked up to find his handsome face across from her, his eyes staring straight between the heads and shoulders of the men seated in the rows ahead of him. She felt a shock of recognition and then quickly bent her head as she struggled with her emotions.

Why was he here if he was a wanderer? Had he stayed all this time, and with whom?

The first song in the *Ausbund* was announced. Paula waited until the men's voices were fully incorporated before she allowed her own voice to rise and fall, following the usual slow rhythm of the plainsong. She was aware of the fact that her heart was beating much too fast, and she felt short of breath, but kept singing to hide this as best she could.

A child began to wail, was quickly hushed by the father, embarrassed at his child's lack of training. The song came to an end, followed by another that was sung at every Sunday church service, "Oh, *Gott Vater, vihr loben dich*" (Oh, God the father, we praise you). She had sung this song as a child and a teenager. It had been sung the day she was married to Manassas and at every church service since. It was familiar, grounding, bringing a sense of belonging and comfort as she sang.

The minister spoke gravely, spoke of hell and eternal damnation through the sins of the flesh, the eyes, the lust of the world and all the things in the world. His gray beard wagged, his eyes flashed fire as he lifted his hands and allowed his voice to roll out across the small group, instilling the fear of God. He spoke of redemption through the blood of Christ, but there were conditions to meet. Obedience to the laws of the church. A plain, sober life. The unworthiness of the human condition made it all seem very hard, like climbing a steep, slippery slope, falling back until the very fires of hell singed your clothing.

Paula's guilt rose with the mighty voice of the minister until her head was bowed and she prayed for forgiveness. She had allowed earthly desires to rule her, so with all her heart, she hoped God would grant her the forgiveness of sins.

There was another sermon after silent prayer, this time preached by a younger man recently ordained. He spoke quietly and hesitated as he tried to remember the German verses he had studied so diligently, and which now seemed to elude him. He struggled courageously on, and with the prayers of the congregation, he brought a sermon that was fairly good and which people appreciated.

Next was a long prayer read from the small black prayer book, another song, and then services were over. Children slipped silently out into the cold, refreshing, slippery outdoors, only to be brought back and seated at the long table with bowls of bean soup. Made of dried navy beans, hot milk, and pieces of bread soaked into the beans and milk, it was a satisfying meal for hungry mouths. Slices of bread, apple butter, red beets, and pickles completed lunch, and no one went home from church on an empty stomach.

Katie Weaver sat beside Paula and whispered, "I wonder who that man is."

"His name is Daniel Miller."

Katie eyed her suspiciously. "How do you know?"

"I was on my way to Henry's when he rode up behind me. He just came over from the motherland not too long ago."

"Does he have a wife and children?"

"No."

Paula's slice of bread turned dry in her mouth, so she took up her knife and spread more apple butter. She felt the heat rise in her face, felt her eyes slide away from Katie's sharp gaze, felt as if she was a rabbit caught in a snare.

Katie noticed. "How do you know all this?"

She felt the noose of the snare tightening and decided to be truthful, place her trust in this dear friend who would not pass judgment.

"He came to check on us during the storm."

"Is he courting you?"

"No. No, of course not."

"You seem ill at ease, Paula. As if you wish he were." She poked an elbow into her side. "I bet you do."

Paula's face flushed and she turned to find the elderly Lydia watching her with the gaze of a hawk about to nab its prey.

How much had she heard? Lydia was like the community's constable, discerning trouble with a sharp instinct and the eyes of a much younger woman.

Paula had never been so glad to be driving home from church, away from prying eyes and the precarious position of her conscience.

Chapter Six

Another light snow fell, enough to make the trip to the barn treacherous. But Betsy took all the barn chores on herself, telling Paula she did not want her to slip and fall. She waved a hand airily, dressed in warm clothes, and slipped and slid her way to tend the animals. Paula was grateful. She might never fully understand her older daughter and there were plenty of times she felt exasperated with her outright cranky ways, but she was a blessing, no doubt.

Paula counted her coins, hoping she could purchase a Sunday dress for Betsy, then set about planning the trip to town. Three weeks and Christmas would be here, so she would need to go soon in order to sew the new dress in time.

She cringed as she heard Dorcas cough. And cough. Then there was a weak cry as the cough woke her. Quickly, Paula rushed to the bedroom to pick her up. She didn't feel hot, so the fever hadn't returned. Paula put honey in hot water, gave her the tin cup, and held her on her lap. She kissed the top of her head where the thin, blond hair always touched a soft spot in her heart. Paula wanted to shield her from the worst of life's barrages, protect her with a fierce love.

She dreaded the coming winter months. The lingering cough was not a good sign. She would stop at Henry and Malinda's on the way to town to get her opinion. She also needed to know if Daniel was there. Surely Malinda had not agreed to take on a boarder, the way her house was packed to the roof with all those children.

Why had he been in church? Would he come to see her again? The unanswered questions burned her heart and mind. She could hardly claim the privilege of being the one who had kept him from leaving and following the old instinct to wander, to ride across the next unknown ridge, and the next.

Who knew if the kisses had meant as much to him as they did to her? If they had, surely he would have stopped by to see her again or at least sent some form of communication. She should never have revealed her fears, the lamentable state of her ongoing childhood superstition. Again, she felt the uncomfortable stab of shame.

Betsy clattered through the door, banging the milk pail against the frame, but didn't spill a drop due to the fact there was very little in the pail at all. If Brown Cow dried up and had her calf in a few months, that meant there would be no milk for Dorcas, a needed sustenance for her. Well, there was nothing to do about that, for sure, so she squared her shoulders and picked up her courage.

"Betsy, today we're going to town," she said brightly.

"We are?"

"Yes. You wash up, and I'll comb your hair, then Dorcas. I'll put the water on for mush."

"It's slippery for you to go to the barn."

"We'll manage."

They dressed, quickly ate the cornmeal mush with milk and molasses, and banked the fire. Holding hands to steady each other, they slid to the barn. Bob seemed eager to be out and about, nickering when they entered through the door.

The sun was shining, the sky was blue, and there was only a slight breeze. The buggy robes were heavy and warm and everything seemed bright and anything possible. The buggy was light, the front of it open, but there was a roof over their heads, so if storm clouds collected they had nothing to fear.

As before, they were jostled about due to the deep ruts in the road, but they made a game out of it to see who could keep from sliding across the seat. They were breathless and laughing as they approached the last hill leading to Henry's homestead, the buildings nestled on the side of Vesper's Ridge, the mound of trees and rocks a protection against the worst of the elements. Their home was substantial, the barn large and built in the best way with the back side against the ridge for better access to the second story.

Henry peered from the open barn door, then hurried out to take Bob for her.

"To what do we owe this pleasant surprise?" he asked, looking at her beneath the brim of his tattered straw hat.

"We're on our way to town. Christmas will be here in three weeks."

"True, true. Malinda has been knitting and sewing day and night."

"I suppose she would have to."

"The children can always look forward to a gift."

Paula smiled at the sight of Malinda's round form appearing on the porch.

"What brings you, Paula? Hello, hello. Give Bob to Henry and come on in. I have fresh gingerbread."

"No, not today, Malinda. I'm going to town. Christmas is coming and I need a few things. I'm worried about Dorcas. Her cough seemed to linger, and I believe it's getting worse."

"Oh," Malinda drew her eyebrows in concern. "You just leave her here. She can play with Andy and Hettie and I'll listen to her cough. Please do. Let her stay here till you come back."

She stepped off the porch, as agile as a much younger woman, her bulk sailing across the snowy pathway without fear. Reaching the buggy, she reached up to take Dorcas, who went willingly, mostly on account of her gentle nature, but also looking forward to her time with little Hettie.

So Paula and Betsy rode to town together, both feeling the relief of knowing Dorcas was warm and safe and being well cared for. Paula tied Bob at the hitching post and she and Betsy stepped excitedly through the wooden door into the dim interior of the general store. A bell tinkled above them and a myriad of scents rushed up to meet them as they greeted Mr. Windsor, the storekeeper, who met them with the respectful half-smile he reserved for all the Amish women who came to his general store. He was half afraid of them, truthfully. Like nuns, they were. Holy or something. Their large black bonnets were drawn well past the curve of their faces and shawls pinned tightly below their chins, flapping to well below their knees. Austere expressions, quiet voices, never laughing. He felt judged by their appearance, as if he was smeared all over with residue of the world, its colors and sins and gaiety.

"Good morning," he said quietly.

"Good morning," Paula answered.

"How may I be of service today?"

Quietly, she reached into the pocket of her skirt. He glimpsed the lifting of a black apron, a slim hand handing him a slip of paper with neat handwriting.

Paula reached up to untie her bonnet, then slid it off her head to better examine the swatches of fabric he would show her. Mr. Windsor was caught quite off guard as he took in the gleaming black hair, the complexion like pale honey, her almond eyes.

He blinked, blinked again, thought, *My goodness. Is this what is hidden behind those bonnets? Well, may the Lord be praised.*

She bent over the swatches, chose a dark red for Betsy, and seemed very pleased at her decision. He gathered the remaining purchases and told her the total, which seemed to please her even more.

"Then, if that is the total, I would like to have two pounds of coffee, and two of sugar if I may."

He was delighted at her obvious joy and hurried away to add them to the paper-wrapped parcel. He placed it in her hands, smiling genuinely.

Paula carefully counted out the coins required and handed him the exact amount.

"May I give the child a treat?" he asked.

"Yes."

Betsy reached out her hand to receive five candies—two red, one yellow, and two green. She held them to her chest, blinked her eyes, and said clearly, "Thank you."

"You are welcome, child. My pleasure. May you both have a good day."

Paula wished him the same, put on the heavy black bonnet, and tied it below her chin, obscuring the sight of her lovely face.

Mr. Windsor found himself watching the retreating figures, thinking that bonnet was like setting a tin bucket on a gorgeous flower.

Strange people, these Amish, but they seemed to be decent builders, farmers, good managers of fields and animals. He'd heard a man named Joseph Garber was building a tannery down by Robinson's Crossing. The county needed a tannery.

* * *

Paula was happy to spend the noon hour with Malinda on the way back through. The older children

were in school, so the house was not as overflowing as
sometimes, when there was barely an empty spot in
which to stand or sit. Paula had said Dorcas would
likely cough through the winter, but she gave her
packets of comfrey and horehound to treat the congestion. Malina waved away payment, saying she'd
love a few loaves of her good bread, though.

Paula wanted to hear about Daniel so badly, but
thought it quite foolhardy to question outright, her
conscience like an uncomfortable burr. Better to
leave well enough alone.

She was about to leave when Malina slapped the
tabletop, asking if she'd heard about Daniel Miller
opening a buggy shop down by Robinson's Crossing.
A hand went to her chest to still her runaway heart-
beats, but she feigned disinterest.

"Really?"

"Yes. He's buying the old Varner place. I heard
he's already hiring stone masons for the shop, so what
does that tell you? He's not an ordinary wanderer,
the way he says he is. He's being too humble. Davey
Easch is going to apprentice him, he made wheels in

Switzerland, but wants to move to Lancaster County. Better soil, I guess."

"I hope he does well. I'd think there would be plenty of trade."

"Most certainly, Paula. Well, if he bought that place, he'll be in our church district. Won't that be nice?"

"Yes, it will be."

Malinda eyed her with too much wisdom and understanding. She placed a hand on Paula's. "Don't forget—someday, you might marry again."

Paula smiled, but retained her secret well, the secret that gave her so much joy—and shame.

He was staying! The thought lent wings to her heart, and on the ride home she allowed her dreams to soar. Why not? Oh, certainly why not? He was here, he was establishing a trade, so perhaps someday. . . .

She was shaken from her reverie by the sight of a dark bird wheeling just above the treetops, then another, and another.

Their cries rose above the sound of the steel wheels on snow, cut into her happiness like the edge of a sword. The ravens had returned to dip below the tree branches, to totter on thin swaying twigs, their horrible black claws clutching, clutching, their thick black beaks opening wide to emit the threatening screeches that sent chills up her back.

One stayed close enough so she caught the all-knowing evil glare of his round yellow eyes. He flapped his strong wings to propel him along in front of them, as if escorting them into perdition.

Paula opened her mouth and screamed. She threatened the powerful black birds with her hoarse cries of fear and panic. She was so caught up in the urge to escape them she could not hear Betsy's anxious cries.

"Go away, you filthy, despicable creatures! Leave me alone! You can't bring me bad luck, you can't, you can't!"

She was crying now, bringing down the reins on poor Bob's haunches who took off at a brisk trot, throwing the buggy from side to side.

"Mam!" Betsy screamed, grabbing the reins out of her nerveless fingers. When she did that, Paula came to her senses, wiped her eyes with the back of her hand, and took control of the reins, but still hollow sobs wracked her body. With one last raucous call, the raven lifted itself above the trees to call for its companions, tilting this way, then another way, as if to show its prowess.

Paula ceased her weeping as they unhitched, rubbed Bob down with good brushes, and fed him hay and plenty of water before walking to the house together. Their outerwear put away, Paula bent to stoke the fire, crisply using the bellows to fan the flames, then sat wearily in her armless rocking chair, drawing wide-eyed little Dorcas on her lap.

"Betsy, let me explain about the ravens."

Betsy listened raptly, commenting occasionally, but seemed to grasp the concept of her mother's fear, nodding her head.

"But Mam, there will always be ravens. I remember Dat showing them to me. He said they're very smart, so perhaps they like people. Tease them."

Paula shivered.

"No, Betsy. They portend bad luck."

"That's just what you believe, but ravens are everywhere. They don't bring bad luck to everyone or everything they see. Surely not."

"Before Dat passed away, I saw them every day."

Betsy bowed her head, plucked at the edge of her chair, her mouth set in the determined way she had. "I don't believe it."

* * *

When there was a knock on the door later that evening, after the sun slid behind the snow-covered mountain, Paula's first thought was the advancing raven. She opened the door to peer into the stern face of Atlee Gaber, the deacon, followed by Davy Easch, the young minister.

"Hello."

"Hello."

"Are the children awake still?"

"Yes."

"Then I would ask you to come to the outside. Little ears should not hear what we have to say."

She obeyed, numb with the cold, stiff with apprehension. She wrapped her arms around her waist to steady the shaking of her body.

"Paula, there are rumors."

There it was, the ravens telling her of this unfortunate occurrence.

She remained still as stone.

"Did you have a young man here in your house for two days and two nights?"

"Th . . . there was a storm. He had to stay."

"This I find hard to believe. A young widow is easy prey to the wiles of a man of disreputable nature."

"So it's true," the minister said quietly.

Resigned, Paula said quietly, "Yes."

"And have you fallen low enough to commit the unthinkable?"

"No."

"He remained circumspect?"

"He did."

"At any rate, you will be expected to make a public confession on the Sunday of our services. You are asked to come to church and let them hear your apology for hosting an unknown man. Do you agree this was a poor display of good judgment?"

"I do."

"Very well. We expect to see you next Sunday. I wish you God's blessing and ask you to be more watchful of the devil's snares from this day forward."

She was shaking badly, her teeth chattering with the cold and the bitter sentence pronounced to her. She had never confessed anything in church, had always felt sympathy for those who did. She fumbled at the door latch, watching the black, wide-brimmed hats fade away into the dark night before letting herself into the warmth of her home.

She was heartsick and felt a deep regret, an overpowering shame. She had not lied. He had remained a gentleman. She was the one who had instigated the kiss. She had longed to be in his arms, but no one could take that away from her. Was a kiss such a terrible thing anyway? Surely a simple kiss was not "the unthinkable" that the minister was referring to.

* * *

She tried to put it behind her, for Betsy's sake, who loved the thought of the approaching holiday. She draped herself over Paula's chair to watch every stitch she put into the new red fabric. They made more cookies, except this time, they were plump, golden sugar cookies, with store-bought sugar sprinkled on top.

The house was warm, the sun shone every day, and Paula decided to invite Henry and Malinda's family over for Christmas Day.

She would butcher the chicken with the broken wing, bake it the morning before, and make *roascht*, the traditional bread casserole with plenty of chicken pieces, onion, celery, and parsley. The hen was fat, so there would be plenty of flavor. She'd make mashed potatoes and rich yellow gravy. Mashed turnips and diced carrots. Plus, they would make a black walnut Christmas cake with brown sugar frosting.

Paula finished the socks, wrapped them in brown paper, and put a peppermint stick on top. She made a new rag doll with the scraps from her sewing basket with brown buttons for eyes and an embroidered nose and mouth. The doll would have a new blue dress and gray apron, yarn for pigtails—yellow yarn, the color of Dorcas's own hair. The new slate was wrapped in brown paper and Paula put a fresh holly branch containing five berries on top, then sat it on the cupboard top to tantalize Betsy, who almost had a fit of hysterics.

She had never had a package that big or decorated so fancy, so she was one hundred percent sure this Christmas would be extra special. Which was Paula's goal. She would focus on the girls and not on her own troubles. She wavered between wishing she had never met Daniel Miller and wishing he would show up at her door. There was comfort in knowing he was actually established here in the community, but it did not mean he would ever court her, or want to marry her.

Oh, she would marry him straightaway. She would.

And no one could take that thought away from her, either.

The thought of the required public confession sent her heart plummeting frequently, but with a prayer for courage, she mostly accepted it now. She felt best being obedient, with all due respect to authority, to be willing to admit mistakes and be humbled. *But oh my*, she thought. What would Manassas have said? Always one who needed a clear explanation of why anyone had to confess, often bordering the line between compliance and rebellion, he'd likely have gone down fighting. But he was not here to protect her anymore. She wondered if the minister had spoken to Daniel, too, but guessed probably not. He was a guest still, not an established member of the church. She hated the idea of him enduring the shame of her confession and hoped desperately that he wouldn't be there that Sunday. She didn't think she'd have to say *who* had spent the night in her home, but people would figure it out quickly enough.

Betsy said the pigs were getting too big for their pen, but Paula knew butchering day was not until after Christmas, when Tobias and Lena Easch, Henry, and Malinda would spend the day helping Paula put up the hogs. A blessing, a pure, undeserved blessing, being allowed to have caring friends who helped her put away a fresh supply of salt pork, sausage, ponhaus, and the good, clean, rendered lard, used for cooking and soap making, breads, and cakes. So if the pigs were very fat, that meant there would be plenty of lard.

Butchering day was special, the scent of fresh meat permeating the whole homestead. Malina was always in high spirits, stirring the lard, saying she wished she could render her own excess poundage.

"An easy keeper, I am. A handful of walnuts will put on the extra pounds. Only one handful of walnuts, you mark my words."

Lena told her a handful of walnuts was a lot of walnuts and Malinda snorted over her shoulder and said she guessed so, for someone no bigger than a good-sized *schnoke* (mosquito), which set Lena to laughing till she wiped tears. The men joked and laughed, delighted in eating the brains fried in the pan, allowed the children to eat the crispy parts, a rare delicacy.

Paula wished she had fresh-smoked ham for Christmas, but knew the *roascht* would be delicious too. What if she invited Daniel? What if she slipped him a note after church, asking him? But of course she wouldn't, even if he was there. Especially not after making her public confession. Perhaps after he saw her chastised in the presence of the congregation, he would never want anything more to do with her.

Well, so be it. Ravens or not, if she remained obedient, God would choose to bless her. This she believed as well.

Chapter Seven

SUNDAY MORNING WAS DARK, GRAY, AND STILL. The air was crisp, wet, with the sure sense of snow in the air. Paula sniffed the heavy scent of the fir trees, the scent she loved so much, especially when the clouds were lowered and the air was still. It seemed as if the deep stately pines were her protector, like grace, sifting the winds of adversity, reminding her there was always the Comforter, the bearer of grace and mercy.

She had slept fitfully and now, on her way to the barn, her eyes felt heavy, so she lifted a hand to swipe at the weariness, leaving her vision blurred. She wasn't sure if having Daniel in her house during the storm was really an outright sin. But her conscience was guided by the ones in authority, and they knew best, so she would give in to the minister's orders if that was what was required to remain an upstanding member of the church. The deep shame she would feel, especially if Daniel was present, was heavy weight on her shoulders as she harnessed Bob.

Betsy was in a mood, sitting stiffly in a corner of
the buggy seat, the lap robe drawn up over her shoulders, glaring out like a baleful cat.

Betsy sniffed at the lap robe.

"This thing smells bad."

Paula shifted the reins in her hands, "Lap robes all
smell bad."

"Why don't you wash it?"

"You can't wash them. The wool is too heavy."

"It stinks."

Paula allowed her that observation without cor-
rection and drove on through the cold, her thoughts
definitely not occupied with the smell of the buggy
blanket. As she stood in the kitchen, the women
all greeted her graciously, always kind to the lonely
widow in the congregation.

She realized she held a special place in the community and was grateful. Everyone shared the garden produce, loads of hay, workdays to cut trees for
firewood—without this she might not survive. But
after today, would her church friends still want to
contribute? They might despise her, think her a loose
woman, unfaithful to the church.

She sat with her head bowed, absorbing very little of the sermon, her palms perspiring, her heart beating too rapidly, leaving her mouth dry. She willed the time to go faster, to get this over with, then willed the clock to slow down, give her more time to prepare herself.

After the final prayer, the minister announced a council after services, meaning the adults would discuss serious matters after the children left the room with a few older children designated to supervise the youngest ones.

As the last song was being sung, Paula felt worse and worse, her heart beating an uncomfortable rhythm in her chest. She sat very still as the children left the room, then dutifully left her seat on the bench to make her way to the minister's bench after they announced her name. She knew Daniel was in the back row, but everything was only a dark blur, the shame and humiliation cloaking her like a dark cape.

After a moment's deliberation, she was asked to tell the congregation of her sin, which she did, quietly. The minister repeated what she had said so all could hear. After that, she was asked to leave the room so the congregation could decide on the proper punishment.

Again, she obeyed, leaving the room blindly to stand alone in the small wash house until the conference came to an end. She looked around, noticing the thick limestone walls. This house was not made of logs the way many of them were, but was larger, with two stories and much larger windows. Ephraim and Annie Stoltzfoos were well to do, had been in Switzerland, leasing a much larger portion of land than others, so here in America they prospered as well. Ephraim was known to pay the passage for people of lesser means, to make a start in America easier.

She jumped when the deacon's wife appeared and lifted a finger to beckon her to return to council with her. Paula was brought back to the ministers. She willingly pronounced her confession, the hope of forgiveness, and the need to be more aware of dangerous pitfalls in the future. The ministers and congregation accepted her words of humility and contrition, a silence falling throughout the room.

Unexpectedly, a voice was heard, deep and sincere.

"I don't think this is right. I am the one who caused this trouble, so I, too, will make a confession."

With that, Daniel rose, made his way to the minister's bench, and sat beside Paula. She felt the nearness of him and her heart swelled. She was so glad to feel his presence, nothing else mattered.

The ministers acknowledged his wish, and he repeated the same German words Paula had spoken, after which they were both admonished to be more watchful as they walked their Christian walk. From here on out, he was expected to stay away from the widow Paula's house.

They were both wished God's blessing. This blessing was spoken in kindness and love, of this Paula felt sure, in spite of having to face the congregation later, feeling the shame of overstepping the church's boundaries.

She couldn't bring herself to help with the tables, unable to hold her head up to face the men, so she stayed with Dorcas until her turn came to eat. The woman eyed her curiously, and Katie squeezed her hand, bringing tears of gratitude to Paula's eyes.

Finally, she could find someone to get Bob and could be on the road home, shut away from prying, curious eyes and judgment.

Daniel had shown his true self by sacrificing himself to stand tall and be by her side. He was a man of truth and integrity. He surely was. A joyful lightness overtook the feeling of shame. Oh, she would marry him tomorrow if he asked. She rode home with her two girls beside her, the dreaded event past, the blessing received.

But when would she get to speak with Daniel again? How? Visits to her house were strictly forbidden. Courting was the only way it would be allowed, and that done in secrecy—not because courting was shameful, but it was tradition to keep it private. Did he want to formally court her?

Paula shivered and tugged at her woolen shawl. The clouds appeared ominous, like bulging gray blankets tossed from one mountain to another, the air sharp and wet, as if the snow was already breathing its portent.

She was prepared for another storm and would rather enjoy the week of Christmas with the two girls, cozy and warm, with plenty of food to eat. She would let go of the thought of Daniel arriving to check on their well-being.

After Bob was safely in the barn and the buggy pushed into its lean-to against the north side, they walked to the house together, Dorcas's little hand firmly in Paula's. A measure of peace and accomplishment followed her, bringing a lightness to her step. She swung Dorcas's hand, smiled down at her.

A shrill cry shattered the stillness and Paula looked up to find the dark shape of a raven perched on the oak tree directly above the house. She stopped in her tracks. Betsy, who was a few steps behind her, bumped into the back of her skirt.

"Mam!"

Irritated, Betsy swerved aside and stomped on without looking back. Another raucous shriek and Paula felt the cry from the top of her head to her feet. She whispered, "Please." She could not afford another display of hysterics for Betsy's sake, so she stood as if frozen to the ground. It was as if the very epitome of evil was launching a bold curse over her own house, bringing death, poverty, accidents, a storm so bad it would topple the house.

"Mam!"

She shook herself.

"Betsy."

"Stop it. Don't even think about crying and yelling. Go get the rifle and shoot the stupid thing. If you don't, I will."

"You can't," Paula whispered hoarsely, still caught in the grip of something she could not control.

"I can try."

Betsy waved her arms, jumped up and down, screeched, until the raven lifted its black wings and moved off through the trees.

"Come, Mam. He's gone. You have to get over your fear. He's no different than any other bird. Just bigger and smarter."

Paula moved as if in a dream, shaken to the core. If a raven chose to go so close to the house, surely there was a special meaning. She trembled to think of the storm's arrival, Dorcas's cough, every calamity happening in the blink of an eye. Her hands trembled as she divested herself of the black shawl and bonnet, then dug the poker in the gray ashes of the fireplace, fully expecting to see the welcome glowing embers. There were none, only the puffs of powdery gray ash.

Immediately, the raven's powers to bring bad luck sprang to her mind. She felt no irritation, only a sense of crippling fear as she set about clearing the ashes from the fireplace, her mouth in a grim, tight line.

"Betsy. Bring kindling in. The smallest slivers you can find."

She obeyed, returning with a handful of bark and thin pieces of wood, which Paula lit with her iron and flint.

The fire in the hearth never went out, through every season; even on hot summer days there were live embers for cooking and heating dishwater.

She shivered.

The house was cold, the dark corners ominous, somehow, but after a small flame licked greedily at the dry kindling, then on to chunks of wood, the light illuminated the room with the help of a few candles flickering on the tabletop. It being the Sabbath, the girls were expected to sit quietly while Paula read to them from the German Bible or told them stories of Bible characters, so the fire was doubly appreciated as they drew their chairs close to its warmth and light.

Dorcas soon fell asleep, tired out from her trip to church, but Betsy listened to each word, trying to memorize the German for the time she would enter school.

They made popcorn, salted and buttered it, and sat together like two young girls, talking and laughing about the things you could read in the Old Testament. It was a time Paula cherished, when Betsy forgot everything rankling her good humor and was an ordinary, sweet little girl of eight.

They did chores together, both commenting on the fact the snow had not yet begun to fall. There was no sign of the raven, which was a calming thing.

Darkness came early, and the evening stretched before them, the time she missed her husband most. They made a thick stew of venison and dumplings, then dozed in front of the fire, their stomachs filled.

Paula was awakened by a firm rap on the sturdy oak door. She scrambled quickly to her feet, felt a moment's dizziness as she tried to focus on the door, but reached it and groped for the handle before lifting it and peering into the dark, cold night.

The only person she could imagine was Daniel, so a quick shock of disappointment washed over her when she recognized one of Davey Easch's boys, the oldest one, she believed it was.

"Why, hello. Do come in."

"*Gūte ōvat*" (Good evening).

A hand was thrust in her direction.

"I was asked to deliver this."

"Oh."

Paula reached for the brown envelope.

"He will send me on Tuesday evening for your reply."

"He?"

"Goodnight."

Paula was left at the open door, clutching the envelope with the sound of a horse's hooves disappearing into the night.

Betsy was sitting up, her eyes wide.

"Who was it?"

"One of Davey Easch's boys."

"What did he want?"

"He gave me this."

She held up the brown envelope, then sank into the armless rocker to open it. She drew out a single sheet of unlined writing paper. Her eyes went immediately to the signature.

Daniel Miller!

Dear friend Paula,

Since we are forbidden to be in each other's company, I believe the only way is to ask if I may court you. I am serious in this endeavor, also having reason to believe you may give your consent.

I would very much like to spend Christmas Day with you, although you may have other plans. I'll be waiting anxiously for Tuesday evening.

In Christian love,
Daniel Miller

Paula slowly laid the letter across her lap, absent-mindedly smoothing the creases. He had touched the paper, this envelope. Had written the words. Oh yes, he had plenty of reason to think she would give her consent. Yes, yes, yes, she would, and gladly. Her eyes focused on nothing, and a lopsided smile appeared on her face.

"Who wrote it, Mam?"

"Daniel."

"You mean, the one who was here?"

"Yes. Him."

"What did he write?"

"He would like to spend Christmas Day with us."

"He doesn't have to. We have all Henry and Malinda's family here. There is no room for him."

"Oh, surely, Betsy."

"No. He's too big. And he doesn't know how to milk a cow or adjust a bridle. Besides, his horse eats too much. He's a pig with hay."

Betsy plopped both hands in her lap, sniffed the air, and fixed a cold, calculating gaze at her mother.

"But I want him to be here."

"That's because you want to marry him. You like him the way you liked Dat. I don't want another Dat. He's not my father."

"Betsy, stop. I said nothing about marrying Daniel."

"But you want to."

Paula was the first one to look away, before realizing Betsy was being obstinate. Children were subject to the parents' wishes, not the other way around. She took her firmly in hand, told her speaking in that tone of voice to her was not acceptable. She would make her decision and Betsy would obey that choice.

Betsy considered her mother's firm tone before saying the raven in the tree meant the letter was trouble, figuring she could frighten Paula into submission.

Paula, however, did not consider the raven and the letter as one. The letter was a miracle, a blessed miracle from God alone. How could she have given the raven enough power to assume there was any bad luck coming in her direction? When the ministers came to her door after hearing the ravens, wouldn't they have appeared anyway, raven or no raven? And tonight, the raven so close to the house had brought only a blessing in the form of Daniel's letter.

Yes, the fire had burned out, but wouldn't it have done so without the appearance of the awful bird in the tree?

She was overwhelmed with love for Daniel, allowing herself the liberty of feeling what had been suppressed in the face of insecurity. He wanted to court her. He wanted to begin a friendship with her, honorably, within the rules of the church. Eventually, she supposed there would be a marriage. Had anyone ever been more blessed? She felt visited by an angel, felt as if she found favor in the eyes of God.

Why had she ever told Daniel she was born under a curse? It had only been the strange surmising of a mother who did not have a healthy mind. She would have to believe this.

On Tuesday evening, her letter was written and sealed into one of the few envelopes she owned. She handed it to the young courier with a sense of great anticipation.

* * *

Paula baked butternut squash pies, golden brown with cinnamon and nutmeg. She made dried apple pies and vanilla pies with heaps of brown sugar crumbs on top. She stored them all on the pantry shelves and started the black walnut cake with brown sugar icing.

Betsy refused to help, saying the only reason she went to all this trouble was for that big Daniel. When that brought no response, she retuned to the part about his horse's bit, till Paula made her go to her room with no dinner. She knew she was being strict, but Betsy needed a good dressing down, she really did think.

Next Paula cleaned and waxed and polished.

The good china plates were washed and dried, then the silverware. So many of her good glass tumblers had been broken on the voyage across the Atlantic, she had to make do with some tin cups.

The next morning she brought pine branches in, wove them into garlands and added sprigs of holly berries, arranging them carefully on the mantle, and then lit thick white candles above them. Betsy clapped her hands about that, newly chastised and in a much better mood.

The barn was cleaned, cobwebs swept, and fresh straw spread in the tie stalls for the visitors' horses. Betsy carried buckets of water from the creek to fill the watering trough, grumbling to herself about Daniel's big horse being a pig.

Betsy had no intention of being won over by him. She didn't care how often she would have to be sent to her room. She had been painfully hungry, though, especially yesterday, so she planned on keeping her dislike of Daniel to herself.

Perhaps, if she was lucky, enough ravens would shriek at her mother and she'd decide Daniel was bad luck. Henry's Ammon said ravens were smart enough to drop stones in a shallow pool to bring the water level up to where they could reach it. They were probably smart enough to realize Daniel was not a good idea for her mother.

Chapter Eight

CHRISTMAS DAY DAWNED BRIGHT AND clear, the snow so dazzling it appeared to be blue on the north side of drifts. The wind picked up pockets of loose snow and sent it whirling away into the trees like restless ghosts of winter.

The raven perched on the closest pine tree where he had a sweeping view of the house, blinked his round yellow eyes, and waited to see if the back door would open and scraps of food would be thrown onto the pure white snow. The yellow light in the window cast a rectangle of light on the ground outside, as if there was a yellow opening in the snow.

Inside, Paula was up and dressed in her Sunday best, a dark blue dress with a black cape and an apron, a gray workday apron pinned over the top. She had taken extra care with her hair and covering, revealing just enough of her gleaming black hair but not too much to appear fancy or too youthful for her age. Her dark eyes shone as she worked, peeling potatoes, mixing the fragrant *roascht*, the chicken being done to golden perfection after roasting very slowly above the night embers. She worked quickly, pulling the tender meat from the bones, cutting it in small pieces to mix with the bread cubes. She smiled at the golden yellow broth, thinking of the fragrant gravy spooned over mounds of potatoes.

When Betsy appeared, she was given prompt orders to go to the barn to get the chores done.

"I have to do your hair when you come back in. Oh, and would you remember to check for eggs, Betsy? It would be lovely to have a few eggs to mix with the *roascht*."

Betsy yawned and cast a sideways glance at her mother. She swiped at her unruly *schtruvvels* of hair, shrugged into her coat, and tied her black scarf under her chin before sitting on the floor to pull up her boots.

"Make sure there's plenty of water for the horses," her mother called absentmindedly over one shoulder.

Betsy didn't feel like answering, so she didn't.

"Did you hear me?"

"Yes."

She slammed the door only a bit harder than necessary on her way out.

Sure enough, the first sound from the surrounding forest was the discordant slash of the raven's call. Betsy stopped in her tracks and put her hands on her hips, her face lifted to the pine tree.

"You old bird!" she called, shaking a fist. "You go ahead and screech all you can."

She imitated the call, over and over, and was pleased to see the great uplifting of the massive wings, even more pleased to see the raven settle on a lower branch and tilt his head to listen to the voice from below.

"What? You're no dummy!" Betsy shouted.

The raven shifted his weight from one foot to the other, his round eyes blinking as he lifted his wings far enough to allow the breeze to ruffle his feathers. But he did not fly away.

Betsy shook her head, then moved on down the slope to the barn. He certainly had no fear of her, but she had better keep this secret to herself. Her mother would not be impressed at the thought of the dreaded bird being so close.

Betsy spent over an hour in the barn, making sure everything was in top shape for the guests' arrival. She poked under feed boxes and swept loose hay to search for eggs, but there were none to be found.

Well, she thought, *nothing to do about that*. Daniel didn't need eggs in his *roascht* anyway.

She was giving one last look to make sure not a wisp of hay was out of place when she heard a stomping, sliding, whooshing sound. The door was flung open and the huge horse and Daniel Miller leading him came right through the door as if they owned the whole barn. She did not move away from the watering trough, but stood as solid as a statue cut from granite, her black eyes never leaving his face. The horse caught sight of her, stopped, snorted, and lifted his head.

"Calm down, Ray."

Betsy's eyes never wavered.

"Ray?"

"That's his name."

"That's no name for a horse."

"Do you have a better one?"

She didn't bother answering his question. "Did you do something about that bit?"

"Not yet."

That irritated Betsy, so she asked how he'd like to go around with a too tight bit in his mouth.

He looked down at this brash child from his great height and thought how she needed a father who taught her a few manners, and right at the moment, he would love to apply for the job.

"I haven't been to the harness maker. I have been very busy."

Betsy wasn't interested in anything he had to say, so she turned on her heel and left through the side door, leaving him feeling as big as a small dandelion. He slipped off the saddle and slid the bridle over the ears before stabling the massive animal. He gave the hourse a forkful of hay and then walked to the house, the one place that had been in his mind for weeks.

The door was opened from inside, and like a vision come to life, Paula stood before him, her dark eyes alive with genuine warmth and gladness.

"Come in, Daniel. You're early!"

He bent low to whisper in her ear, his breath a benediction, his nearness her undoing. "I couldn't wait one more hour."

She blushed and lifted her face to give him the full benefit of her radiant smile. He answered with a smile of his own, his eyes telling her how much he had missed her.

Dorcas ran to her mother and hid her face in her skirts. Daniel bent to shake her thin white hand, but she quickly retrieved it before hurrying her face back into the skirt.

"Come, Daniel. You must warm yourself and have a cup of coffee. I have plenty in the pot."

"That will be wonderful, Paula. You spoil me."

If you only knew how gladly I serve you, Paula thought, as she turned to find a clean mug. He noticed her trim waist, the swan-like neck that rose above her black cape, and thought how he would love to place a hand on both. But he knew that time had not yet arrived.

"The mug is hot. Be careful," she said, as she placed it in his hands.

"Thank you, Paula. My, it smells good in here. Do I smell *roascht*?"

Paula was delighted. "You do. Imagine. Are you fond of it?"

"My favorite."

Betsy appeared, reaching behind her to button her Sunday dress, the new red one her mother had just completed. Paula caught sight of her, smiled, and told her she was very pretty in the new dress, and that the fit was perfect. Instead of the smile that should have appeared, Betsy frowned and said the button-holes were way too small for the buttons.

"They're new, Betsy. They'll grow bigger each time you push a button through."

"What's for breakfast?"

Daniel laughed, ashamed to have come quite this early. Paula assured him everything was alright, but Betsy fixed those unfathomable eyes on him and said nothing.

Toasted bread and tea wasn't much of a breakfast after all that time in the barn, but Betsy knew to eat the bread without creating a fuss.

Daniel offered to help and proceeded to push the drop leaf table to the wooden table, and Paula brought the snow-white linen tablecloth. She placed a hand on the cloth, smoothing it over and over, saying how soft it was, then picked it up to breathe in the scent of it. Daniel watched her and thought the contour of her cheek was much softer than the tablecloth.

"I'm so glad we brought the things we did in the trunk. I was afraid the passage across the Atlantic might be too expensive with two large trunks, but it was worth it."

"The trip was harrowing for me. I'm not much of a sea man, and to be held captive by that creaking, moldy vessel for all those weeks . . ."

He shook his head at the memory.

"Manassas was quite ill for a week. But I found the heaving of the restless water fascinating. There is a sense of adventure about the sea. You're never quite able to comprehend its moods, its great secret. I spent hours on deck, writing poetry to the ceaseless waves and the cry of the gulls. And to think, one misstep, a small plunge, and the great swell of water would claim your life. A watery grave."

She gave a small shiver.

"I would like to read what you have written."

She glanced at him, shy now. "Perhaps someday."

The good china was set on the white cloth. Twelve place settings. The men and children would eat first, the women serving them, after which they would wash the dishes, reheat the food from the serving bowls, reset the table, and finally indulge in the good food at their leisure.

Paula combed and braided the girls' hair, then told Betsy to bring their black pinafore-style aprons. Betsy frowned and said she didn't want to want the black apron, that it covered all of the red dress except the sleeves. Paula marched her to the bedroom and told her to put it on without further ado.

The Henry and Malinda family, as Paula called them, arrived in a great flurry of cold air, red cheeks, and loud voices. They carried containers of cookies and a great yellow spice cake, the smell of horses and the outdoors permeating every corner of the small house. It felt as if they brought the very spirit of Christmas with them. Betsy and Dorcas were swooped up in the colorful medley of children being unwrapped from scarves, boots kicked into corners, hats hung haphazardly on an available hook, others flung into corners with boots.

Betsy forgot for the moment about her distaste for Daniel and was soon teaching Simon and Dorothy the art of playing cat's cradle with a length of twine.

Malinda caught sight of Daniel and shook a finger in his direction.

"You are not supposed to be here!"

He grinned.

"This time I am."

Bewildered, she looked from Daniel to Paula. Henry stood beside his wife, his jaw dropping open at the thought of how daring Daniel was to defy the orders of the church in this way.

"But . . ." he spluttered. "You promised."

"I can't believe you did this, Daniel."

"I have done it the proper way this time."

Henry and Malinda did not understand, till the oldest girl, Bertha, smiled at her flummoxed parents and said, "Perhaps they are courting."

Then Malinda's mouth opened in disbelief. She tried to speak but burst into tears, threw her apron over her head, and left the room for a breath of air on the porch. Henry bowed his head and said reverently, "*Bedenklich, Ich vinsch euch da saya*" (Wonderful, I wish you a blessing).

Bertha grinned shyly and the older children giggled and poked a finger in each other's ribs as they chortled with the newly discovered secrets, their father warning them to keep it just that, a secret.

Paula moved from fireplace to table, her face flushed with happiness, her cheeks like rosy apples. But if you looked closely, there was a remembered sadness in the depths of her eyes, something no one knew except for the one closest to her heart and mind.

Daniel pondered this as he visited with Henry at the far side of the table. When he recognized the moments of darkness, he berated himself for having moved too fast, too soon. And yet, she had been glad to see him. He was sure of that, though he couldn't say the same for Betsy.

They talked of growing wheat, the most promising crop of the growing community, and the need for a good buggy maker. Daniel said he was learning week by week, but the wheel making was actually much harder than he anticipated.

The house was filled with so much noise and movement, mingled with the smell of potatoes steaming on the dry sink. Malinda was wielding the wire potato masher like a club, her substantial girth weaving and bending through the sea of excited toddlers and older children. The gravy was given another stir, the lid taken off the turnips and carrots to check for doneness, and Paula nodded to Lydie and Bertha to begin pouring the cold water into the glasses. Glass dishes of applesauce, pickled beets, and sour green pickles added color to the table, as did the pot of butter and wild grape jelly.

Plates of sliced sourdough rolls and thick slices of bread were set at each end before steaming platters of *roascht* were added alongside. Paula and Malinda added serving dishes of potatoes with browned butter running down the sides of the fluffy mound, gravy in bowls with ladles, turnips and carrots with a brown sugar glaze, and everything was set. Daniel and Henry were followed by the oldest of the boys, according to age, until the twelve places were filled.

"All set?" Henry asked.

When there was no answer, he took it as an affirmative, dipped his head, and began the traditional silent prayer. Everyone followed suit, Malinda and Paula standing back, their heads bowed, hands clasped respectfully. After everyone raised their heads, Henry said loudly, "Everyone fall to and help themselves. If you don't get enough to eat, it certainly is not the good cook's fault."

Plates were heaped, spoons and forks applied, with the women hovering, helping the small ones, buttering bread, refilling water glasses, bringing more gravy, more *roascht*. Daniel ate prodigiously, his appetite matching his size, with Henry's well-rounded girth running a close second.

There were cries of appreciation at the appearance of the cakes, the pies, the plate of cookies. To have cake was a rare treat, especially with icing on top, but to have two different kinds of cake was almost too much luxury.

Daniel said quietly he'd never eaten a better vanilla pie, his favorite, and Paula was immensely pleased, although she hid it well. Malinda asked immediately after whether they liked the yellow spice cake and was rewarded with resounding approval. The children declined cups of tea or coffee, and Daniel was thoughtful enough to remind Henry they should leave the table to drink their coffee, the women and little ones were hungry.

So they bowed their heads again and thanked God for the food in their stomachs before leaving the table. Malinda and Paula began to clear the table while Lydie and Bertha poured boiling water in agate dish pans, followed by cold, then shoved lye soap in one and began to wash.

There were plenty of mashed potatoes and *roascht*, but the gravy was getting low, so Paula added a bit of water. They reset the table for seven, then filled the water glasses, served up the food, and asked everyone to be quiet again.

"It's our turn to pray," Paula said softly.

Everyone held still, coffee cups were lowered, and children's play hushed while the seven heads were bowed, raised, and the eating began. Malinda piled her plate high, lowered her head, and shoveled the food into her mouth at an alarming rate.

She laughed halfway through, said she'd skipped the porridge this morning and was especially hungry. She ate three slices of pie and a thick slice of spice cake, sighed, and stretched before asking for the black walnut cake. Three cups of tea later, she was still jolly and still gossiping . . . but "in a nice way," she said.

Bertha and Lydie were large girls with strong arms and wide hips. They joined in as their mother related bits of community goings-on and ate slice after slice of cake. Paula could not help but notice the buxom Lydia eyeing Daniel repeatedly, simpering and giggling at her mother's words.

But he wrote me a letter, she thought. *It's me he wants.*

She was cloaked in gladness, an emotion so rich and deep and appreciative she felt she had never been blessed like this. When they bowed their heads a second time, she closed her eyes and thanked God especially for the letter Daniel had sent to her.

Dishes were washed, leftovers put away, and presents were exchanged. Betsy was pleased with her new slate and Dorcas squeezed her little white rag doll and laughed aloud, the thin, tinkling laugh that often ended in a cough.

There were hard candies and oranges, a treat so rare they saved them for later, to be eaten one section at a time.

German hymnbooks were brought out, with Henry leading the first song in a quavering baritone.

Many voices chimed in until the small house was filled with the sound of the carols, peace, goodwill to all men who rejoiced at the Christ Child's birth.

Next, Paula chose *"Freue dich velt, der könig kommt"* (Joy to the world, the Lord is come). She started the hymn in her clear, strong voice, the rest chiming in as the familiar tune began, the beloved German words evoking fond memories of times in Switzerland, where many of their friends and relatives remained. There, the wealthy landowners distributed gifts of meat and cheese, jugs of ale, the hearty English fare they always looked forward to for the holidays.

Here in America, there were no wealthy landowners to bring anything. They were responsible for their own land purchasing, the buildings they erected, everything. But the group was prospering, the men working from sunup to sundown, fiercely adhering to the goal of thriving off the land to establish farms and raise families who would keep the ways their fathers had taught them.

When the singing came to an end, Henry said very solemnly he thought it would be nice to have the story of the Christ Child read from Luke. Malinda nodded, pious when need be, and said, "Yes. Elam, go get Paula's Bible."

She sat with head bowed, waiting for the Scripture story to end. She felt the sting of irritation when Henry's voice rambled on, clear up to the time Jesus was twelve years old and his parents lost him in the temple. This wasn't church, it was Christmas, and she thought she had heard Paula say something about popcorn balls and cider. A glass of cider would be delicious after all that pie. Oh, and she forgot to tell her about Sam Gnage's son William, the one she always felt would ask Lydie someday.

When Henry's voice finally fell silent, he closed the book with a snap. She reached across Bertha and tapped Paula's arm.

"Paula."

"Yes, Malinda?"

"Didn't you say you made popcorn balls?"

"Yes, I did. And I have cider. I'll get it now."

"No. Wait. Sit. I forgot to tell you about Sam Gnage's William."

Paula wrinkled her brow, tried to think who Malinda meant, but shook her head.

"Well, he asked Rachel Zug, and she said yes. Now he's courting her and she's way too young and not much to look at."

"Mother!" Lydie gasped, appalled.

So Paula was laughing as she stepped out to the lean-to for the cider where it was staying cold up against the house where the split wood was stacked.

She jumped when Daniel came around the corner carrying a load of wood for the fireplace.

"Oh!"

"Sorry, Paula, didn't meant to scare you," he said, smiling.

"It's quite alright."

Quickly, suddenly quite shy, she bent to insert a finger into the handle of the crockery jug. She heard the wood hit the ground, then froze as she felt his hands on her waist. Slowly she straightened, turned, her eyes going to his, questioning, her heart skipping along too fast.

"Paula."

That was all he said, but her name was a caress, spoken in a voice filled with awe. She found his eyes with the same message, and she drank from the adoring gaze, allowing it to fill up all the empty spaces the sadness of Manassas's death had created.

"May I stay after they leave?" he asked, his voice thick with emotion, with the great love he wanted to profess.

"Yes! Oh yes. Of course. I was so hoping you would want to."

This generous woman was all he could think of. This graceful, generous woman who brought so much to his life. He thought he had a fulfilling life before, and he had found adventure, excitement, but nothing came close to this.

He felt weak with his love for her, as if his knees had turned to maple syrup.

He bent to pick up his wood, and she to the cider jugs, but both hearts were singing with the promise of being together that evening. The promise of the time when all the unspoken words could be spoken without fear of refusal.

Chapter Nine

THE LAST LITTLE GUEST WAS BUNDLED INTO warm clothes and carried through the cold to the waiting sleigh, cries of "Goodbye," "Good Night," and "Thank you for everything" echoing across the snowy expanse as the eager horses pawed the frozen snow. As the sleigh slid silently into the night, the trees on either side swallowing them up, Daniel stood with Paula in the light of the door, waving and calling. They turned together to scoop up shivering Dorcas, closed the door firmly, and surveyed the mess. Paula lifted her hands, saying, "I hardly know where to begin."

Betsy looked up from her place by the table, the new slate in front of her, waiting till everyone left to bring it out, to use the new chalk.

Words were held back until Betsy yawned and said she was going to bed. Dorcas was already half asleep with both her new and her old rag doll.

Prayers had to be said, so they knelt side by side in front of wooden chairs while Daniel read from the German prayer book, his deep voice rising and falling. Betsy was grateful to snuggle beneath the heavy sheepskins, her eyelids heavy as she allowed her mother to braid her hair.

* * *

"It's too soon, Daniel." When they were alone, the words tumbled from Paula. She felt it was too soon, much too soon to feel the way she did. She was afraid of allowing herself to fall in love, to care for another person the way she cared for Manassas.

He tried to reason with her, unable to see it her way.

The house was cleared of Christmas leftovers, the puddles of melting snow by the door mopped up, the floor swept. They drew chairs close to the fire, grateful for the leaping flames, the heat and coziness.

Paula twisted her hands in her lap, her eyebrows raised with the weight of her fear and foreboding.

"Is it the curse your mother spoke of, Paula?"

"No. Well, maybe. Yes, perhaps it is."

Daniel stared into the fire, his long legs stretched before him, his gaze seeing nothing as he pondered her words.

"Do you still see the raven?"

"Sometimes."

"And does he terrify you as before?"

"Not if I reason with the truth. If I tell myself God allows things to be or not to be, a raven shrieking or not. But still, in the back of my mind, I calculate what happens, separating bad luck from ordinary events. I'm so afraid if we move too fast, the raven will call and . . ."

She hesitated, took a deep breath before plunging ahead.

"And you will take a tumble from a horse and die. I can't go through it a second time."

He sighed, gathering his thoughts. "Those ravens and bad luck have nothing to do with anything. But my word will never persuade you, since you insist on clinging desperately to your mother's upbringing. So if you want, I'll go away and not bother you with my presence, give you space and time to try to overcome your fears."

"No. Please, Daniel. I don't want you to. I was so very happy, so looked forward to being alone with you tonight, until the sleigh with Malinda and the family slid away in the dark and I imagined it going over a cliff, ravens in the trees."

He shook his head in disbelief.

"Don't allow those morbid thoughts. Think of the light on the sleigh, the sleepy children. Malinda falling asleep contentedly as the horses find their surefooted way home. Henry at the reins."

She closed her eyes, sighed a deep sigh.

"Oh, I do so want to be rid of these thoughts."

"You will be. There's a verse in the Bible saying, 'Perfect love casteth out fear.'"

"But how can we know we have perfect love?"

"You can start with me," he grinned.

"But we just met, Daniel."

"I know."

"You know."

"I do. But that has nothing to do with it."

Very slowly, he slid from his chair to kneel by her side. His arms encircled her, his heavy forearms in her lap. She stiffened, unable to comprehend the meaning of this.

His words were thick, garbled with the magnitude of his emotion. "Paula, I have never met a woman who could keep me from wandering. I have searched for a partner, I'll admit, and saw plenty of attractive girls, not all of them Amish. The world was my palette. I could paint it with whatever colors I chose. Nothing ever held me, except the great American land, the mountains, rivers, towns. But ever since I saw you struggling through the snow, I haven't even been able to contemplate the thought of leaving you. I love you, Paula."

She drew a sharp breath.

He changed positions, knelt in front of her, his arms dropping away. Gently, he took her fluttering fingers in his own.

"I'm asking you to honor me by becoming my wife."

She breathed out, lowered her eyelids as her head fell on her chest. She tried to silence the pounding of her heart, quell the enveloping fear of allowing another love into her life.

"Daniel," she whispered.

He looked into her troubled face. Slowly, she reached out to place the palm of her hand against the side of his face. He placed his hand on hers. The logs fell in the fireplace, sending a shower of sparks up the chimney, and still they remained motionless.

"I will marry you if you'll help me with my greatest weakness."

"God help me, Paula. I will do anything in my power to win your hand. Please say you love me, too."

She smiled, a beautiful smile of acceptance, her dark eyes sparkling in the firelight.

"I do love you. Daniel, I do."

In each other's arms, time stood still. There was only the nearness of one another, the newfound knowledge of knowing the love they felt was shared. Their lips met in a long and tender moment of love, until Paula drew back and said they must talk. She wanted to share so much more of her life with him, wanted to hear so much more of his.

The words that came from her that night were revelation to Daniel, an insight into the reason for her strange fear of the ravens.

He pictured the cold stone walls of the village in Alsace, a stern-faced, dark-clad figure hovering over her, threats, whispered pronouncing of myths and superstitions. Often left alone, brutally lonely and forsaken, her father a timid shadow of a man who lived in fear of his own wife, yet would never condone leaving her because of her insanity.

Married at sixteen against her mother's wishes, the bishop pronounced them man and wife, and urged the young Manassas to take her to America where she found a reasonable happiness, two healthy girls. But she was left reeling with the deaths of the three she had lost.

Daniel held her hand and listened attentively as the story poured from her like a spring bubbling eternally from the mountainside. The beatings, the times she'd begged her father to intercede on her behalf, the poor man never daring to lift a hand.

There was a soft cry from the bedroom, followed by the hacking cough so typical of Dorcas in the wintertime. Paula got up and went to her, comforted her with a cold glass of water, and tucked the heavy blankets around her again. When she returned, Daniel was pouring hot water over mugs of tea leaves, the vanilla pie on the table.

"Only two slices left," he said. "And I'm so hungry."

She smiled, but sank gratefully into a chair, stirred the tea, then deposited the leaves on a plate.

"I'm glad you feel comfortable in my house. So glad you're here with me tonight. I feel as if a heavy burden has been lifted already, as if every word I have said to you was cleansing. I need you to be with me, Daniel, someone who does not judge me for all of my strange thoughts."

"Oh never. Never do I look down on you. Look. I have a plan. I think we'll give this a bit of time, but only a bit. Not too long."

He laughed, took her hand, and held it to his dry, warm lips. She smiled into his eyes, alive with the emotion he felt for her, the longing to be with her every hour of every day. His heart sang with the happiness he felt for his future with her.

"For one thing, we have a formidable opponent in one little girl named Betsy. She simply doesn't like me."

"What? What are you saying?"

"I had a rather cold reception at the barn today," he said, then grinned.

"I'm sorry."

"No, don't be. It's quite alright. She's a very independent child who is not afraid to speak her mind. And I just happen to be the unfortunate person she has no use for. I can't imagine what her response will be when we tell her about us."

"She knows. She's much too smart for her age. She knows why you show up. And she's going to do her best to get rid of you."

Paula shook her head, ashamed to say this.

"So, we'll see if I can win her over. What do you suggest?"

Paula thought for a moment.

"I honestly don't know."

"Well, I will ask God for help. It's late now, dear Paula, your eyes are heavy with sleep, and I will take my leave."

The actual leaving did not take place for another hour, but the security of their love was firmly established, with plans for a wedding in early spring. She and the girls would move to Robinson's Crossing to live in a stone house, with neighbors, as a buggy maker's wife. Paula's eyes shone with the joy of the thought of a new life with Daniel.

She loved the idea of neighbors close by, a cluster of houses that was a small village. Betsy going to school, making new friends. If she allowed herself to feel the happiness, dispel the dark clouds that threatened on the horizon, it was too much to take in at one time.

This was a Christmas like no other, the gift of his request. The love he had for her. To be his wife.

But still, she knew, the Christ Child was the greatest gift of all, far above and beyond any mortal gift of love.

* * *

Betsy was not happy with her mother's newfound love, or the plans for her future. Children were taught to be silent, to accept the will of the parents, but for her, this was an impossibility. She listened stone-faced as her mother spoke. She took her fork and cut the remaining crust of bread on her plate into tiny bits. Her mother added bits of helpful information, trying to elicit the response she had hoped for.

"Why, Mam?" she asked, finally.

"We don't always want to be alone, just the three of us. The people from the church have to share their food, come help with firewood. I am a widow, and you are my poor widow's children, so if someone like Daniel asks if I will be his wife, I think I should."

"You think you 'should.'"

"I mean, I want to. I love him and want to be his wife."

"How can you, if you still love Dat?"

Betsy was slowly working up her anger, Paula could tell, so she told her very firmly that Dat had died two years ago, that this was her choice and Betsy was expected to accept her mother's decision. After that, Paula got up to clear the table and told Betsy it was time to do chores and that the matter was closed.

Betsy stomped off the porch and down the icy path to the barn, her face lifted, watching for the raven. Perhaps there was still a chance to scare Daniel off if she could keep that bird around.

She didn't see him this morning, but as she entered the barn, a plan formed in her mind. She would keep bread crusts and scraps of apples and lure him closer. She was the one who gave all the table scraps to the pigs, and they wouldn't miss a few crumbs here and there.

So her heart was cheered as she cleaned stables, forked hay, and threw ears of corn to the horse, a bit of oats and corn to the cow, and corn fodder to the pigs, who grunted and squealed as they rolled around in it. The rooster strutted beside her, dashing forward to peck at any fallen morsel.

The barn was warmer than the freezing air outside and the animals were friendly, so Betsy dawdled. She made a thorough search for eggs but had to give up eventually. There were none. She knew the days would turn longer, which would have all the chickens laying an egg every day.

She swept the earthen floor with the reed broom, set it in the corner, and surveyed the interior of the barn. The animals were all chewing contentedly, their jaws working, the chickens pecking at the corn she had scattered. The cow had gone dry, so there was no milking to be done, which meant no milk to drink or use for cooking, either. But it meant a new calf, which was even better than milk.

She let herself out and searched the treetops for the raven, but could only see and hear the frenzied twittering of flocks of sparrows and the "too-weet, too-weet" of the red bird, so she let herself into the house. She spent the morning writing letters and numbers with her mother, the new slate taking away the foul mood about Daniel and the unthinkable marriage she was expected to accept.

But when she went outside after dinner, she heard the questioning raven's call, and another one answering. Quickly, she turned and went back inside, asking her mother for a crust of bread.

"What do you want with it, Betsy? We just ate."

"Just a little treat for the nice birds. They get hungry this time of year too."

It was true, Betsy reasoned. The ravens were nice, most likely. It wasn't her fault exactly if her mother was imagining her feeding the chickadees or blue jays rather than the ravens that she hated.

If she was lucky, Betsy thought, the raven could be trained to stick right around the house, and if Daniel was as superstitious as her mother was, maybe he would stay away. The rooster down at the barn didn't like him, either, so what the rooster didn't accomplish by a good flogging, the raven's screeching just might do. Maybe it would give him the willies and he'd leave her mother alone.

Paula allowed Betsy to take the bread, but not without trepidation. She crossed her arms tightly across her waist and stood by the south window to watch her stalwart daughter go down the path to the barn, stop halfway, and lift her face to search the treetops. Just then, Dorcas started crying and Paula rushed away from the window to check on her.

* * *

Betsy was in her element. She could tell the one bird was fascinated, probably the one who'd watched her before. The other bird lost interest and flapped away, shrieking a warning to the curious one.

From the top of the bare chestnut tree, the raven perched uneasily, stepping from side to side, lifting his wings, turning his head to peer down at this person who seemed to want something from him. He opened his beak, emitted the raucous cry of his species, and was promptly answered with one from below.

Betsy lifted her hand, the bread crust extended, an offering. The raven cocked its head one way, then another. Finally it left its perch and hopped to a lower branch.

Betsy held her breath.

She was disappointed to see him flap his wings and fly off through the trees, but she kept the bread crust in the pocket of her dress as she went to get the wooden sled from the barn. All afternoon, she trudged up and down the steep hill by the pasture, packing down the loose snow, cutting out a trail for the sled.

The afternoon sun melted it just enough to make an icy crust, and by supper time she was flying down the hill at breathtaking speeds. Over and over, she rode the sled down the hill until her legs could barely carry her up, dragging the wooden sled. She was hungry, and still had all the chores to do, so she put the sled away, went to the house, and sat on the braided rug inside, her face tanned even darker from the brilliant sunlight on snow.

Betsy put on dry socks, warmed her hands by the fire, and went to do barn chores. Paula offered to help, but Betsy said she would do it.

"You stay here and make supper. I'm so hungry."

Paula laughed at her and said Betsy would sleep well that night, with all the fresh air and exercise.

Betsy saw the raven again, this time in the maple tree by the barn. She tore the bread crust in half, then in half again, and lay a portion on the top of the fence post before entering the barn. She scolded the pigs, the way they'd spilled their water trough over the corn fodder, lifting the heavy thing with their strong pink snouts.

"You're going to be butchered soon, and it's a good thing. You're getting too big for your breeches."

She worked hard, shoveling the mess into the wheelbarrow, dumping it on the manure pile outside. She stopped to watch the mourning doves picking at the wisps of hay around the pile. They were pretty birds, gentle, making a cooing, clucking, warbling noise, like water over pebbles. Perhaps she should tame a dove, so much nicer than that crazy raven.

When she got to the fence post, the bread crust was gone and the raven was screeching at her from an even lower branch. She nodded her head, knew exactly what he wanted, having tasted the bread crust and finding it delicious.

"Alright, bird. You can have more, but you'll have to come closer."

And so the game continued all week until the black bird was on the path within feet of Betsy, sidling his body along, watching her warily without daring to come closer. It was a fun game for her as she harbored no fear of the clever bird at all. She became more and more intrigued, in fact, thinking how he could stay around the house like a watchdog, shrieking a warning the minute anyone arrived.

* * *

Sure enough, the raven called, hopping from tree branches to the tips of swaying pine trees in the stiff breeze when Daniel rode up to the house Sunday afternoon. If he didn't know about Paula's fear, he might never have noticed the fuss the lone raven created, but now, he watched it with a certain amount of annoyance. The bird acted as if he knew to stay around, as if he owned the place, really. Almost like a barking dog.

He said nothing about it to Paula all evening, afraid to raise another discussion of what the raven meant to her. He wanted things to be normal, to discuss only the future and how much he looked forward to being with her every day. Betsy was pouting, while Dorcas allowed him to hold her on his lap, giggling and laughing as he told her little stories. She was a sweet, winsome child, one he could love as easily as he loved Paula, but he had no idea how he would ever win over Betsy, especially on an evening like this.

He tried. "Are you enjoying your new slate?" he asked, as he watched her concentrate on the letters she was writing.

When there was no answer, Paula said, "Betsy, your manners."

"Yes, I am," she said quickly.

Daniel caught Paula's eye, and they both smiled. She shook her head very slightly, to let him know how bad she felt, but Daniel mouthed an affirmative reply.

From the table Betsy said, "I saw that. You're making fun of me."

Caught off guard, both of them felt like traitors. Would Betsy's actions be the bad luck Paula was so afraid of? Would she, like the raven, discourage any close relationship and future with Daniel?

Chapter Ten

WINTER DAYS WERE NOT IDLE DAYS FOR Paula, even if it meant longer nights of rest, sleeping quite soundly under the heavy weight of the sheepskin comforters.

The temperature dipped to ten degrees below zero. The logs creaked in the night and the interior of the house was so cold there was frost on insides of the windowpanes in the morning. She slipped out from beneath the covers and shivered out of the long flannel nightgown and into her blue everyday dress, leaving her long, black hair in the braid she always wore at night.

She tiptoed across the freezing cold floor to the hearth that still held a bit of heat, took up the cast iron poker, and stirred up the gray ashes, watching for the welcome red embers. A bit of kindling, a few puffs from the bellows, and a flame leaped up, licking at the dry wood. Next, she added a few thick chunks of wood, then swung the kettle over the crackling fire to heat water for washing.

She rubbed the frost from the windowpane to see the brilliance of a fiery red eastern sky. *More snow*, she thought. *Red in the morning, sailors take warning.* She smiled to herself, glad to acknowledge the fact she was not a sailor but had both feet on dry land in a free America, blessed by God, where she planned to stay for the remainder of her days with Daniel.

The heaving seas had fascinated her, spending all those hours on deck in the bracing salt air, and she had fancied herself brave on the creaking little vessel as it rose on swells and dipped into troughs between waves. Manassas was always below deck, dreadfully ill with the seasickness. But she had helped him regain his strength and together they had made their way in the new world, with God as their help.

That all seemed far away since Daniel had come into her life. She hoped this was alright with God, that he could bless this union as he had blessed her with Manassas. Only sometimes did she feel guilty, as if she was being unfaithful to his memory. But she reasoned that there was nothing in the Bible saying one shouldn't remarry after the death of a spouse. She smiled again at the memory of Christmas, the glow still alive, still as bright as the eastern star.

She would find a sprig of mistletoe today, surprise Daniel with a belated Christmas kiss beneath the mistletoe, for good luck.

She was interrupted by the sound of padding feet and turned to find Betsy rubbing the sleep from her eyes as she made her way across the cold wooden floor to the hearth.

"Betsy, it's still early. Are you feeling well this morning?"

"Yes. I'm just done sleeping. My bed makes me tired."

"Well, Betsy dear, you just cuddle up by the fire. Here is a warm blanket for you. I'll do the barn chores this morning. I need a breath of fresh air. I feel as if I've been cooped up long enough now."

Betsy yawned tremendously, rubbed her eyes, and drew the blanket over her shoulder. Should she say something about the raven? He was bound to watch her and screech the usual message to herald his approach. She decided to let it go. Her mother needed to grow up sometime and she might as well start today.

Paula waited till daylight, then dressed in her heavy work coat, scarf, and boots, pulled on a pair of mittens, told Betsy to listen for Dorcas, and let herself out into the biting cold, a mittened hand going to her mouth as she breathed in the frigid air. She made her way carefully, watching for patches of slick ice.

She froze in her tracks as the shrill cry of the raven sliced through the morning light. Her head swiveled from side to side as she desperately searched the trees for a sign of the dreaded marauder.

She thought of those birds as cold-hearted murderers of her peaceful existence, destroying her faith, her forgiveness of the past, slashing to pieces every courageous day she had accomplished since childhood.

A dark movement in the fir tree caught her eye.

There. He was sitting much closer than she'd thought. He was in plain sight. Paula froze, her mind spinning as she struggled with the taunts of her inner cowardice, the voice repeatedly telling her this bird was sent to remind her of who she was, an unlucky woman born instead of the son her mother craved.

She stomped her foot, waved her arms, but without the all-consuming panic she'd felt so many times before.

"Shoo! Shoo, bird! Go away!" she shouted.

The bird tilted its head, stared at her as if he meant to speak to her.

She felt fresh chills of terror start in her spine and spread to her shoulders, felt her chest thick and heavy with fear.

"Shoo! Shoo!" she screamed, waving her arms, but when the bird remained on its perch, the head turning from side to side, showing no fear, panic overtook her and she ran. She slipped and slid, running blindly to the barn where she burst through the door and fell in a heap on the straw-littered floor, shaking with heavy sobs. Finally, the time had come, the time when all the horrors of her past in Switzerland had caught up to her in the form of this black bird who was sent to remind her of her misplaced birth, her disappointment to her mother, and lack of God's blessing.

She did not feel the cold damp of the earthen floor or hear the rustle of the chickens who walked over to view this curious sight. It was the rooster who dared lower his sharp beak and peck through the woolen scarf on her head. She gave a small shriek and reached up a hand to protect the spot the rooster had pecked before scrambling to her feet, suddenly empowered by a shot of raw anger. She searched wildly for a broom, a rake, anything to run after that dreadful, cocky rooster, who was decidedly not going to finish the work the raven had started. She could find neither one, so she dashed first one way, then another, chasing the squawking chickens to the top of the wooden gate by the cow's pen. Around and around she went until the rooster was cornered. He stood, eying her with malevolence, his yellow eyes round and unblinking, lifting his feathers ferociously.

Paula's breath was coming in short gasps.

"Flog me," she hissed. "Go right ahead and try it."

As if he understood, the rooster attacked, the dusty wings flaying her unprotected face, the sharp spurs catching the woolen fabric of her coat.

She reached blindly, caught one wing, felt the rake of the feet scrabbling for a hold, but held on grimly. She put the strength of her strong arms into pinning the rooster against a log wall, which took away the ability to flap his wings. Quickly she grabbed the mottled, waxy legs, cutting a deep gash in her hand on one of the spurs. No matter, there was no time to be wasted. It was the soup pot for the rooster.

The pigs squealed in fright. Bob the horse darted from one side of his pen to another, snorted, and pawed the ground. Chickens ran everywhere, squawking senselessly, but Paula didn't pay them attention. She grasped the tips of the rooster's wings and heavy yellow legs, turned him upside down, and carried him up the slippery path to the house.

The raven hopped down to the lowest branch and made a show of settling himself before lifting his beak and emitting an awful cry. Paula had no time to listen to the silliness of the raven; she had a more important mission to accomplish.

She yanked open the front door and yelled for Betsy, who appeared immediately, her eyes wide. She rarely heard her mother raise her voice, and when and if she did, there was cause for alarm.

"Get dressed. I want you to hang on to the rooster while I get a bucket of boiling water."

Betsy ran.

Paula laid the rooster, helpless now, on the chopping block, and showed Betsy how to hold the feet and pin the head. No one else could have done it at her age, but Paula knew she would do it.

One hefty whack with the axe and his head flew off the block and into the snow, leaving a red stain where the blood drained. When the rooster ceased to move, Paula picked up the headless body, grabbed the feet firmly, and doused it in boiling water, swishing it around and around by the heavy, yellow feet, the long dangerous spurs lifeless now.

"Why, Mam?" Betsy croaked, her voice hoarse, her breath coming in gasps. She had never seen her mother quite so upset.

"He flogged me for the last time, Betsy," she said grimly.

She lifted the great, heavy rooster from the bloodied water, a cloud of hot steam rising in the cold air, the smell of blood causing Betsy to take a few steps backward.

With her bare hands, Paula began tearing at the soaked feathers, yanking them out by the fistful.

The wings were spread, each feather giving way under the pull of her strong fingers, until the large rooster was completely plucked, as bare and pimply and hideous looking as anything Betsy had ever seen.

Paula laid the plucked bird in the clean snow, then grabbed the bucket and tossed the grisly contents into the underbrush.

"We'll have coyotes here tonight," she told Betsy.

In a big agate dishpan, she cut the rooster down the middle, reached expertly into the cavity, and felt around, locating the spot she needed to pull out the entrails intact. She saved the gizzard, the heart, and the liver, then put the rest in the bucket along with the yellow feet and wing tips.

"There. Now take this out and dump it where I dumped the water."

Betsy did as she was told, wrinkling her nose at the warm odor.

Paula cut the rooster into pieces and put them in a cast iron pot with fresh cold water, salt, and a few flecks of red pepper before hanging the pot on the hook above the fire. She wiped her hands on a dishcloth before getting down the great cast iron frying pan and slicing corn meal mush. She added a dab of lard, then set the slices to frying on the grate above the fire, below the boiling pieces of rooster.

"I'm hungry, Betsy. I wish there were eggs in the barn."

"There won't be for a few more weeks," Betsy answered.

"Well, we'll be happy with our rooster stew, won't we?"

Betsy didn't answer.

"That raven is going to be the next one to be put in a pot," said Paula, her voice low, menacing. "Screeching at me like that."

Betsy looked up in alarm. "What?"

"I don't like the ravens, you know that. I have to stop being afraid all the time. So I'll start shooting them."

"No!"

Paula looked at Betsy. "Why not?"

"Because I don't want you to. I'm taming the raven with breadcrumbs."

"Betsy! You can't do that!"

"Why not?"

Paula shook her head. Why would her daughter want to do anything like that, knowing the fear Paula harbored? She never could understand Betsy, but to go against her mother's wishes in this bold manner was unthinkable.

"No, Betsy. I won't allow it."

"He's quite nice, Mam. He's a funny bird. He knows when it's me going to the barn. I'll have him eating from my hand soon."

"No, you won't. I forbid it."

"Why?"

"Because I am afraid of them."

"You won't be once you get to know them."

Paula said nothing to this.

Finally Betsy blurted out her plan. "If I can keep the raven around, it'll scare Daniel off. I don't need a father."

"Betsy! You're not thinking straight."

"What? Of course I am. I told you. I don't want Daniel for my father."

Paula lowered her eyes and sighed deeply, suddenly exhausted from the morning's drama. She knew she'd need to take one day at a time, leave it to Daniel to work things out with Betsy. She decided the best thing was to leave the subject of the raven for now. She knew Betsy would continue to tame the raven, whether or not she was forbidden to do so.

* * *

Dorcas smiled happily as her mother picked the meat from the rooster's bones. The smell had awakened her and made her mouth water, but the cornmeal mush and fried bread had been good for her breakfast.

She knew the chicken and *knepp* (dumplings) for their supper would be even better, with tender chunks of potato, carrot, and onion.

She clapped her hands when Paula offered her the heart and liver, which were very good with salt. They were all happy when Dorcas had a good appetite, so the house was filled with the golden sunlight through the windows, the rich smell of the rooster's meat, and the lisping voice of little Dorcas playing with her two rag dolls, her stomach full. Betsy ate the gizzard, even the tough membranes, pronounced it delicious, and went out to finish the feeding her mother had not accomplished.

* * *

Without the rooster, there would be no baby chicks in the spring, but Betsy figured her mother had over-looked that point. If Daniel kept up these visits with the intention of marrying her mother, well then, he could bring them a rooster. It was the least he could do.

She spent most of the morning until lunchtime persuading the raven to come out of the tree to the snow-covered ground about three feet away.

He shifted his weight from one foot to the other and turned his head sideways. The light caught the golden color of his eyes, the blue and purple over-tones of his black feathers. *Nothing wrong with this bird, not a thing*, Betsy thought.

She needed a name for her new pet, so she called him Jehosophat, which was a long name, a mouthful really, but she liked the sound of it.

* * *

Sure enough, Daniel showed up after dark on Sunday evening, creeping in so no one could see him, not even Jehosophat, which irritated Betsy so that she stayed in the bedroom with the covers pulled up over her head.

She heard their voices sometimes and wasn't surprised when her mother showed up at the doorway, asking her to please come join them for popcorn and hot cider.

"Did he go home yet?" she asked, twisting around to get her face from under the covers.

"No, of course not," Paula said, her voice barely above a whisper.

"When he leaves, I'll be out."

She lied to Daniel that night, saying Betsy wasn't feeling well. Daniel watched the tension in her face, saw the evasive eyes, and decided the best thing was to let it go.

He'd never walk away, never. If Paula agreed to be his wife, he would learn how to deal with Betsy. His face took on a relaxed expression, his eyes going often to Paula's troubled eyes. After Dorcas was put to bed with her sister, who had now fallen into a troubled sleep, he asked her to tell him what was troubling her. For a long time she would not, but when she saw the love and concern in his eyes, she told him everything, from the call of the raven, to killing the rooster, to Betsy's taming of the raven, how she wanted to be free of superstition and fear.

"Do you think killing the rooster was symbolic? As in killing of a bad omen?" she asked, her voice quavering, her eyes darting from one side of the room to another.

For a long time Daniel was silent, carefully weighing his words. When he spoke, he assured her he would not take her fears lightly, but she needed to put her whole heart into seeking God's love, which was the only way she could possibly overcome it.

"But killing the rooster was brave, wasn't it?"

"Oh yes. Of course. But you can't do a deed your-self and say it will overcome adversity. We wrestle not with flesh and blood, as the Bible says, but with spirits and powers in the air around us."

"But that is what I am afraid of. I can't overcome them with my weak and frightened mind."

"No. Not with your faith, either. If we have faith to move mountains and have not love, we are worth nothing."

"I love you, Daniel," she said suddenly.

"Yes, you do. Of which I am eternally grateful. But you need to love God first and foremost."

"He took Manassas, and for what reason?"

Quite unexpectedly a rush of understanding came to Daniel. She had never accepted her husband's death, in spite of assuring those around her how it was God's will for her life, his time was up, it was all in God's hands. Likely she had been taught this, had heard it countless times, until it became a traditional saying, but one that held no power to overcome the obstacles grief and sorrow presented.

But how to tell her?

"We hardly ever have a reason. God's Spirit, the Comforter, moves among us, and we don't have to know why. Our faith doesn't have to understand."

She seemed absorbed by his answer but remained pensive, withdrawn.

"So I don't have to know why the raven follows me around?" she asked finally.

"No. If you didn't think the raven was bad luck, wouldn't he still be there? In your mind, he would be no different than any other bird."

"I want to believe that. Actually, I was close to believing it. Then came the horrible screech on my way to the barn, and I was just like a child again. I feel trapped by my fear and I cannot find my way out."

"But you will."

Their time together was tender that night, almost sacred, a time of finding there was nothing they could not overcome together. They even laughed about Betsy taming the raven and naming it Jehosophat.

He rode home with the moon as his guide, his hands and feet numb with the cold, a small price to pay for the love of a woman like Paula.

* * *

The month of January proved to be a hardship with frequent snowstorms and crippling cold, the house almost buried beneath drifted snow. Daniel fretted and worried, pacing his own stone house with the sturdy chimney, hoping Paula and the girls had sufficient firewood and a way to get to and from the barn to keep the animals fed. He chafed at tradition, keeping him from marrying until a proper period of courting had been completed.

He saw no sense in it, leaving Paula to herself. When he thought he would go mad with the arrival of another storm right on the heels of one that deposited a foot of snow, he decided to try and risk a trip on horseback. But he was defeated after mile or so, his horse falling repeatedly into unseen gullies, wallowing bravely, sweat darkening the thick winter coat, his eyes wide with fright and exhaustion.

He kept the fires going, worked on buggy wheels with the help of the man who'd sold him the business, but lost his appetite for food or company, so riddled with anxiety he could barely sleep. There he'd been telling Paula to set aside her fears, and here he was, put to the test like never before.

Did the raven's presence bring the storms? It was a ridiculous thought, but it was hard not to believe in bad luck just then.

When the kindly bishop snowshoed to his shop, he decided to tell him about his predicament and accept the outcome. He voiced his story without embellishment, told it simply, how he would like to marry the widow Lantz and found it hard to leave her alone in the raging winter storms.

The bishop eyed him with keen blue eyes, his cheeks ruddy with the cold. He accepted the cup of tea, grimaced as he blew on it to cool the hot liquid, and slurped loudly before setting his cup on the tabletop.

Gruffly, he reminded Daniel how unusual it was to speak of these matters before the engagement was announced formally in church.

Daniel felt humbled, chastened by the solemn admonishment. Yes, he knew, but he was desperate.

Like the sun appearing after many days of gray clouds, the bishop's eye twinkled, bright as diamonds.

"But I think perhaps excuses could be made. Your eyes give away the worry about her well-being, which is a good thing. A man's eyes are mirrors to his soul. So if you have a place to hold the wedding, we can announce it in two weeks. Storms allowing, you can marry the following Tuesday, with the approval of the ministers, I believe."

Daniel sat very still, but in spirit, he threw his arms around the bishop.

Chapter Eleven

THE STORMS PROVED TO BE A MONUMENTAL test for Paula as well. It was a struggle to get to and from the barn, and she didn't like leaving Betsy in charge alone in the house with Dorcas. But it was often too wild outside to allow Betsy to go alone. Often it took most of the day to bring in enough wood to keep the fire going and to get enough melted snow for the animals to drink. In the midst of high winds and whirling snow, the chimney suddenly would not draw, so there was nothing to do but brave the elements to find the problem. She used every ounce of her strength to put one ladder against the house, sweep the snow she could reach, and hook the second ladder across the peak of the roof in order to find the problem. The house was cold, the fire banked to ashes, as Paula struggled to reach the top of the chimney. There she found branches lodged across the opening, the snow clinging to the obstruction until it was efficiently blocked. A few pokes of the broom handle and the whole mess fell down the chimney, bringing Betsy's belligerent voice from below.

Well, her fingers and hands were numb with the cold, her legs trembling with fright and exhaustion, but praise God, the opening was clean. She could go into the house and start a roaring fire, which was a real blessing. She searched the sky for signs of a letup, but all around her there was only the cold, gray whirling void of snow. As she struggled to put the ladders in the woodshed, she thought of the deer, the poor starving animals who would not be able to find the necessary sustenance. It made her feel better for having shot and killed the two nice fat does she had skinned and butchered, salted, and cold-packed. It meant life for them, for her and the girls, and for this, she thanked God for giving her these animals.

They would survive these storms, but every hour of the day she thought of Daniel, how his love would pull her through any hardship until the lovely days of spring when they would be married.

When she entered the house through the back door, Betsy was huddled in a blanket, wearing her coat and scarf, Dorcas beside her, with the pleasant expression she always wore. Betsy, however, was outraged, her brown eyes hooded with anger.

"I hope you know that mess of snow and twigs killed the fire dead," she snapped.

Cold, tired, and at her wit's end, Paula was in no mood to shoulder Betsy's ill-founded resentment. Dripping melting snow all over the floor as she shrugged off her outerwear, shivering in the cold house, she snapped.

"And if that whole mess would not have come down the chimney, we could not start a fire and would freeze to death. Would that suit you any better?"

Betsy was speechless for a moment, shocked at her mother's sharp tongue and lack of empathy.

With that, Paula raked furiously at the cold gray ashes, shoveled them into the hood, and opened the back door to set it in the lean-to, now packed with blowing snow. Despair washed over her. How were they ever going to get enough wood inside if this storm kept up? For a moment, she felt real fear, the kind of fear where the possibility of one's demise seems a reality. She was one woman, alone, responsible for the well-being of her beloved daughters, all she had left of Manassas. And where was Daniel, the one she needed so badly at this moment? To see his big, solid form come through the doorway would be as welcome as the glowing sun, chasing away the vehemence of this awful storm. But she had no way of knowing about his welfare, if he was safe and warm in his own house or if he had taken unnecessary risks.

And so she turned to God and felt comforted.

A roaring fire, scrubbed floors, porridge in the cast iron pot, mugs of tea with honey, and the storm seemed to lose its power to frighten her.

She prayed, she got down the black German *Schrift* (Bible) and read comforting passages aloud to Betsy and Dorcas, words of encouragement from King David in Psalms.

The porridge was hot and thick without milk, but it was food for their empty stomachs, and no one complained. She set some of the salted venison to boiling, softening it to make a stew, then got down her darning and prepared to sit by the fire to rest and to warm herself, having been chilled to the bone.

Would she really have to survive this awful winter alone? Unthinkable, having Daniel here, but how long could they find their way to the barn if there was no letup?

"Mam. I'm not going to stay alone in the house any longer. You have to take me and Dorcas to the barn."

"Betsy, Dorcas cannot go outside. Her lungs are too weak."

As it was, the storm intensified as the day wore on, so that Paula staggered backward by sheer force of the wind when she tried to open the door. It was all she could do to close the door and bar it safely before gasping, "Oh my!"

Betsy stared at her mother with a strange expression. She would never give in to her pride, never admit how fragile they all seemed, but for an instant, she knew the only thing that lay between freezing to death and life were the four log walls with the roof on top, and the crackling of the fire in the fireplace. She bit her lips, her eyes growing large and dark with unnamed fears.

"The animals will have to do without tonight. We cannot go to the barn."

"We have to, Mam."

"We can't. We are defeated. They'll live. They'll just be very hungry and thirsty, especially the pigs."

* * *

That day and night were unforgettable. The roaring, howling, swishing sound pressing through the walls was like a ferocious monster chewing up the little log house. The roof might lift with one final gust of destroying wind, or the glass panes of the windows shudder and sliver into a thousand pieces. It was hard to find comfort or stay calm in the face of one of the worst possible storms, no matter how often she prayed or read from the Psalms.

But in the morning, the stillness awoke her. For a wild moment she forgot where she was until the blessed sound of silence wrapped itself in the quiet, peaceful embrace. She shifted beneath the heavy covers, stuck one bare foot out, then another, before sliding her body out as quietly as possible. Dorcas moved from her stomach to her side, coughed once, then went back to sleep.

"Mam."

"Yes, Betsy?"

"Is the storm over?"

"I believe it is. Go back to sleep. I'll get the fire going."

Betsy mumbled something Paula could not hear, so she slipped into her dress, stockings, and shoes before stepping out to start her day.

* * *

The sun shone, the wind stayed calm, and in the blinding light of the snow, Paula and Betsy shoveled a path to the barn. The world was a brilliant scene, everything muffled by the fresh layer of snow, drifts as tall as Paula, the evergreens bent heavily by their encumbrance of snow. Everywhere birds twittered, finding food in the pinecones, or pieces of bark, a few buds on bushes, anything they could find to stay warm and alive.

Betsy stopped, her face lifted to the sky.

"No sign of Jehosophat," she said.

"No. Wonder what happened to him?"

"Maybe he starved."

"Oh, I would hope not."

"Mam! What did you just say?"

"Well, it's not that I like the bird. But it's a cruel way to die for any living creature."

They both looked to the window where Dorcas sat patiently, watching their progress to the barn. She had assured them she would stay by the window till the shoveling was done, a brave, winsome child, who at a very young age thought of others before herself.

Paula would always struggle to understand how two sisters could be so very different.

Once the path was cleared, Paula went inside to bundle Dorcas up so she could go to the barn with them. Now that the wind had died down, some fresh air would do her good. They were greeted by a cacophony of belligerent voices, the animals' thirst driving them to anxious squeals, neighs, and lowing. They quickly shoveled another path to the creek, broke through the ice with the heavy ax, then slipped and slid, hanging on to the wooden bucket as they made their way back to the animals. They worked together, hauling water to fill the trough.

One by one the animals drank their fill, the sloppy pigs spilling half of theirs into the muck, the sheep dipping their heads daintily. Paula ran a hand across the dusty wool covering their bodies, dug her fingers into it, and thought of the good quality woolen clothing this would make.

She loved the hours at the spinning wheel, singing in rhythm to the whirring of the wheel, watching the good wool being spun to thread.

She rubbed a hand across Bob's sleek neck where the winter hairs lay clean and smooth beneath the heavy mane, listening to the small gulps as the cold winter traveled up through his neck. A faithful horse was worth his weight in gold, a good strong companion to pull the buggy or the plow.

"Mam! Come quick!"

Dorcas's high voice broke into her thoughts and Paula turned to find her younger daughter bent over a pile of corn fodder in the farthest corner of the barn.

"An egg!"

Sure enough, there lay a brown egg, large and perfect, a sight to behold for someone so hungry for the goodness one egg could provide.

She would bake a small pound cake with one egg.

Dorcas smiled proudly and carried it very carefully back to the house where Paula made a big breakfast of fried cornmeal mush, fried bread, and stewed apples, then washed dishes, set the house in order, and proceeded to bake the precious pound cake. Betsy sat at the table with her new slate, quietly concentrating on the forming of letters, when they heard the first raucous cry of the raven, very close.

Betsy lifted her head.

"Mam," she cautioned, then ran to the window. "He's here, on the porch," she hissed. "Jehosophat."

Paula stood by the table, frozen for only a short time as she wrestled back her old fears. She felt her breathing increase, the dull pounding of her heart, and thought, *No. This is only a bird. One of God's creatures. Since the raven has been here, Daniel has been here, too. I love Daniel, and am blessed by his love, his asking for my hand in marriage. I love Henry and*

Malinda, my girls, and all those who live in the hills of
Berks County.

With this love, I can overcome my darkest fears.

Betsy said softly, "Come here."

So Paula went, amazed to find the intelligent creature sashaying across the swept boards of the porch,
strutting as if to put on a show.

"You know what he wants?" Betsy whispered.

"Bread?"

She nodded.

So Paula went to get a few bread crusts and Betsy
cautiously opened the door, inch by inch, as the raven
tilted his head to one side to watch if anyone would
produce the bread. When Betsy appeared, he lifted
his wings only slightly before hopping playfully. He
blinked his eyes, then opened his great beak. Paula
braced herself for the dreaded cry that could easily rip
apart the fragile shell of her courage, but none came.

Betsy was delighted.

"He's laughing, Mam. Jehosophat is laughing,
he's so happy."

One bread crust after another was devoured hungrily. Betsy stepped out and extended her hand with

a very small piece held between her thumb and fore-finger, which put the raven into a frenzy of strange maneuvers.

Dorcas burst into a high, tinkly laugh.

"Funny, funny bird," she lisped.

And Paula smiled.

Betsy wheedled and begged, sat back on her haunches in the freezing cold, waiting patiently. The raven turned his back, pecked at the snow, exactly like a pouting child who wanted his mother to think he didn't care if he wasn't allowed to have a cookie.

Just when Paula was ready to open the door to tell Betsy it was too cold to sit out there, the raven stepped sideways, sidled over, and in one swift move, took the bread as delicately as a much smaller, more timid bird. Betsy lifted eyes wide with amazement. Her eyes met Paula's, and between them, a mutual understanding arose, as if Betsy was leading her mother into strange new territory where there was nothing to fear.

Another bread crust, another display of feath-ered wings lifted, dancing, and head swinging. When Betsy had fed him the last of the bread, she re-entered the house, shivered, then clapped her hands triumphantly.

"Mam, you see?"

And Paula smiled a tremulous smile and said she did see.

Before the day was over, they heard shouting voices and hurried to the door to find quite a sight— two huge black horses hitched to a wooden bobsled, steam rising from the sweating horses, and bright blankets and an array of people, all sorts and sizes of children and adults.

Malinda waved a mittened hand and bellowed a cheery greeting, while Henry hopped off the sled, slipping and floundering in the deep snow, before falling flat on his face, the children shrieking with unabashed glee.

When he regained his footing, he was covered from head to toe in the thick, powdery snow.

"Dat is a snow man!" the children hollered.

Malinda whooped and laughed, climbed down off the bobsled, lost her footing, and fell flat on her stomach also, much to the delight of the rest of the children. When she regained her footing with the help of her snowman husband, there was more hilarity, the woods echoing with the shouts and cries of delighted children.

When order was restored, the cry of the raven echoed through the evergreens, followed by showers of snow from the branches.

Paula watched, amazed at the acrobatics of the large black bird, as if he was happy to encounter this chaos.

The house was filled with snow melting into puddles, cloaks, shawls and bonnets, hats, coats, and mittens. Malinda was never happier than surrounded by her family and good food and visiting or having visitors. She had brought a large container of sugar cookies and one of popcorn. Paula took the kettle and filled it with water before putting it back on the hook.

A knock on the door went unheeded until one of the children asked everyone to hush.

Paula went to see who it was, the blinding sunlight obscuring the tall form in the doorway.

"Hello, Paula."

She gasped and gained her composure, before saying quietly, "Is it you?"

"It's me. Probably not a good idea to arrive when you have company."

"Oh, but it is," she whispered.

"You're well? You got through the storms alright?"

"I'll tell you soon. Not really alright. The chimney was clogged."

"Paula."

He only spoke her name, but the care and concern were all she needed to hear to know nothing had changed. Everything, the promise of a new and secure future, was still the same. She had to turn away to hide the rush of emotion.

The afternoon was spent with Henry and Malinda, an exchange of interesting conversation, which included community news, something Paula was hungry for. There was the news of those who became sick, and how sick, what it took to get them back to normal health. Malinda had news of the doctor falling through the ice on the creek, his feet close to freezing before he reached the safety of a home. She was always at odds with the good doctor, telling him where she thought he went wrong with various treatments, even though she had no education. He thought his thoughts about the bold and enterprising Malinda, but being the well-trained and polite person he was, he chose keeping all this to himself while Malinda rambled on and on about the doctor's misfortunes and mistreatments.

Henry dunked a cookie in his cup of tea, chortled, and spoke up quite firmly.

"Malinda helps herself to a large serving of *schadenfreude* every once in a while, as far as the doctor is concerned."

"No, Henry, you know that's not true."

But his statement proved to be the turning point, and the conversation was steered in a different direction. A traveling preacher was wreaking havoc in the Stoltzfoos family, persuading the newly married John and his wife of the weakness of their faith. He claimed no one could know for sure that they are saved, that you could do no more than hope you could be good enough to enter into the pearly gates. This led to an intense debate about the power of Christ on the cross. Daniel and Henry were good conversationalists, both well learned in the way of Scripture, which Paula found extremely interesting. But she couldn't help being pleased to hear Henry announce the fact it was time to think about getting on home.

She was ashamed of the intensity of her feelings, the need to tell Daniel everything about her time apart from him. So she asked Malinda to stay awhile longer, and was rewarded by a hand placed on her knee, a look of so much love in her eyes.

"Now, Paula, we would, but there is livestock to take care of, and the trail is dangerous in the dark."

With much ado, a flurry of goodbyes and best wishes, the bobsled slid away in the bright afternoon sunlight, leaving Paula to stand alone on the porch waving goodbye, an acute sense of loss invading her normal good humor.

Why couldn't he have stayed? It was all Henry's fault, persuading Daniel to ride along behind the sled.

She turned back and let herself in the door, closed it behind her, and felt the wave of loneliness wash over her.

"Good. He left," Betsy commented.

"Not just him. They all left together," Paula snapped.

"Well, I sure hope you're not planning on marrying him anymore. The raven was on the porch."

Paula looked at her, then burst out laughing.

"Betsy, what does the raven have to do with it?"

"He's scary. He brings bad luck."

This from the same child who had earlier worked to convince her mother that the raven was just a friendly, smart bird.

"Betsy, Betsy."

Paula smiled, thinking of Jehosophat and how her own daughter was taming him with the intent to scare off her future husband.

It began with a chuckle, a rumbling, cleansing sound that shook her chest, shook her stomach and continued until she was laughing out loud, and Betsy gave her a questioning look.

And still she laughed.

"What?" Betsy asked finally.

"Oh you. You and your raven named Jehosophat."

She wiped her eyes, took a long cleansing breath. Oh indeed, indeed. You could weigh life on the scales of good and evil, but wasn't it love that weighed the most? Wasn't it love that clunked the scales to the bottom?

Yes.

Yes, it was. All things could be overcome by the power of love, the vital, living waters whose beginning and end were Christ. The Heavenly Father who bestowed all good and pure gifts in abundance.

Chapter Twelve

PAULA AWOKE TO THE SOUND OF DRIPPING eaves, an unaccustomed warmth surrounding her. At first, she seemed baffled by this, till the thought of a January thaw entered her mind, and the thought of Daniel being able to navigate his way to her house brought a swift joy.

All that week the sun shone and temperatures mellowed, with the snow visibly decreasing, a sure sign of his arrival that Sunday evening.

She sang as she washed windows, hummed beneath her breath as she poured the hot water in wash tubs. She lifted her face to the sun and praised God in her soul as she pegged the steaming laundry on the line. The surrounding forest echoed her praise in birdsong, the twitters and warbles, the high cackle of the woodpecker an accompanying symphony.

And there it was.

The raucous cry. She put in the last of the clothes-pins, pressing down hard on the wooden peg, the strong wind whipping the pillowcases and towels away from her. She stopped, her gaze roaming the treetops, until she spotted the large black bird settled on one of the branches of the spindly elm by her wash line. He held very still, his head occasionally swiveling from side to side, watching her.

Paula steadied herself with a deep breath.

"Well," she said aloud. "Well."

The raven eyed her. He blinked quickly.

"Jehosophat. What a name Betsy gave you."

He seemed to agree, hopping from one foot to another, lifting his wings. As if to see what he could accomplish, like a bold schoolboy who needed to try his teacher's patience, he flapped his wings and settled on the wash line post, then bent his head to peck at a wooden clothespin.

"Hey, you!" Paula shouted.

Jehosophat looked like he was laughing at her. He opened his mouth wide, though no sound came out. Then he pecked at the clothespin again.

Paula stopped in her tracks and thought how amazing that a wild raven would sit on a wash line post without fear, displaying a mischievous personality.

Surely they were intelligent birds. She wanted to see if she could do what Betsy did with bread crusts, so she entered the house and found a few before going back outside. She was disappointed to find him gone.

She searched the trees but saw nothing.

"Well, Jehosophat," she said softly.

She was startled by a dark blur to her right.

There. He had been sitting on the roof, or the chimney top. The raven settled gracefully on a bush by the door, then hopped off to the ground, one eye staying on her.

"Here."

Paula squatted in the snow, held out a crust of bread. The raven hopped away, then sidled back, his eyes swerving from the crust of bread to her face and back again. She held her breath, did not move a muscle.

He was very close, so close that Paula could see the expression in his eyes, and it was not evil. Alert, alive, smart as a whip, but not evil.

When he dipped his head as if bowing, then made one swinging motion with his beak, extracting the bread crust from her thumb and forefinger, she gasped in surprise, then laughed aloud as he gobbled up the treat in a few quick shakes of his head.

"You are funny, Jehosophat," she said. "Here. Have another one."

He strutted over, and in the same quick move took the second one, lifting his wings and flying off with it.

"You could at least say thank you," Paula called after him.

Then she stood, watching as he propelled himself higher and higher, away across the surrounding fields to a secret place only he knew about. And she felt a sense of loss, wondering if he'd return for the remaining crust she held in her hand.

Well.

No use wasting good bread, so she bit off a part of it, chewed, and swallowed. It was good, so she ate the rest of it and told Jehosophat they had a mutual meal, a communion, and now she would always understand him to be a wild bird, a large, black raven with a sense of humor. Betsy's pet. No symbol of fear or evil, of this she was certain.

* * *

What a story she had for Daniel, and with gladness he listened. He was taller and even better looking than she remembered him to be from his last visit. How could this man really mean it when he said he counted the hours till he could see her, and that he would swim an icy river to get to her . . . which had almost happened, the creek overflowing its banks, the melting snow adding volumes to the already swollen water.

His horse had been surefooted, an amazing feat, crossing that water. He peeled off sodden shoes and socks, his large feet encased in a woolen blanket by the fire, Betsy wide-eyed and speechless for once in her life.

"I rode hard after crossing the creek," he said. "I was afraid of frostbite in my feet and legs. I need to stay healthy if I want a wife and two daughters soon."

He smiled at the girls, receiving a smile from Dorcas in return, but a stony unforgiving glare from Betsy.

"You aren't my father. You won't ever be, either."

"That is alright. We'll just live together and stay out of your way. I was hoping I'd have help in the buggy shop, but if you don't want to do that, then I guess you'll have to go to school. The schoolhouse is only a few hundred yards away from my . . . our house."

If this got Betsy's attention, she certainly gave no sign.

Paula was furious, but patiently asked Betsy to wash up and get ready for bed. Betsy did what her mother asked, but grudgingly, with happy little Dorcas following on behind, prattling away in her sweet baby voice.

When they were alone at last, Paula apologized for her behavior.

"Paula, we knew we were going to have this."

"It's just inexcusable."

"No. She's been through a bad time, losing her father at a young age, so we need to have patience

with her. I think she'll be pleasantly surprised to find
how happy she'll be living among others in the little
village, going to school."

"I hope you're right."

"You'll see."

* * *

They were married when the onion snow melted into
the bursting tree buds, when the air was sharp with
remnants of the winter's north wind, but the sun
shone pleasantly, warming the limestone walls of the
Yoder home where Sunday services were being held.

There was no wedding, only the usual services, but
they stood before the bishop and were pronounced
man and wife in the sight of God and man and were
given the blessing of Abraham and Isaac. Paula was
a widow, so there was cause for a solemn occasion, a
service not given to undue gaiety and laughter. This
was the custom, but Malinda and Henry left services
early, went home, and prepared a huge wedding supper, complete with a frosted wedding cake.

There was a roast of venison, a turkey stuffed with onion dressing, a baked ham, and sweet potatoes. There was pepper slaw, pickles and red beets, apple-sauce and baked beans. There were canned peaches and a warm vanilla pudding. The whole house was filled to the brim with food and guests Malinda had taken on herself to invite. She didn't care if she was going against the rules or not; Manassas was dead for two years now and Paula deserved this time of rejoicing.

Oh my, but they made an astonishing couple. So dark haired and dark eyed.

Malinda stopped frequently to wipe perspiration or tears, her white Sunday handkerchief coming in handily at times like this. Just such a nice couple. Such a blessing. She could feel the love and happiness throughout the house. But that Betsy. She needed a round of firm discipline. That one did certainly need it. My oh.

* * *

Daniel sat in his chair at the end of the table, Paula close beside him, and thought how he had never known happiness such as this. To be joined to someone like Paula was an undeserved blessing, a grace imparted to him by God alone. He thanked God at the beginning of the wonderful wedding meal and afterward. He touched Paula's waist, marveled at the softness of her, the sweetness of her presence, the wonder of a woman God had designed to fulfill the time of a man's stay on earth. He prayed fervently that He would multiply his days until he was old, that he could grow old together with Paula, the love of his life.

And Paula mirrored the happiness and gratefulness in him, content to feel the assurance of what God had wrought. She included the friendship of those around her, the caring and love Malinda had put into the wedding supper. They all helped clean the dishes, then sat together by the fire and sang German wedding hymns of praise.

Dorcas sat on Daniel's lap, her eyes growing heavy as the fire warmed her little body, and when she fell asleep, he looked at Dorcas the way a father would smile down at his sleeping daughter. Malinda caught this look and tears of joy sprang to her eyes.

Wunderbahr. Preiset den Herren! (Wonderful. Praise the Lord!)

* * *

They moved to Daniel's house when the snow lay in patches, the swollen creek had receded, and forsythia burst forth in a blinding display of yellow flowers. Violets lifted their faces to the sun and brilliant green showed in all the bare fields, the earth singing as it sprang to life.

The stone house at Robinson's Crossing was so much bigger and better than her humble log house— so much so that Paula felt guilty.

She didn't tell Daniel, but only prayed she would not become haughty.

Betsy, however, had no intentions of making life easy for Daniel, so this kept Paula humbled, the way she stalked around on stiff legs, did what she was told out of a sense of duty and nothing else. She never spoke to Daniel, no matter how he tried to draw her out.

But, oh, Paula loved the house. Built of gray limestone, with longer, wider windows and deep windowsills, horsehair-plastered walls, and shining oak floors, it was, quite simply, too much.

She told Daniel. He gazed deeply into her soft brown eyes and said it was a pleasure, a gift to be able to provide a house for her, and she deserved every day she spent in it. It was like ascending a long, winding staircase, taking one step at a time, allowing herself the thought of enjoying lasting happiness, until one day she reached the top, spread her arms, and embraced the winds of change. Her soul sang with a new song when she lay beside Daniel at night, when she rose with him in the morning, and when she spent every hour of every day knowing God was the One who was omnipotent, who had the power to bring happiness or unhappiness, sorrow or joy.

* * *

When Daniel worked in the buggy shop, his strong arms bending the wood, forming wheels and doors and shafts, he became increasingly aware of a very small shadow hovering around corners and doorways.

Just when he thought he might catch the shadow, it disappeared, until the next time. One day, he called out, "Betsy?"

There was no answer, and after that, no shadow for a long time, until gradually, it began again.

"You're like the raven, Betsy," he called out.

Taken completely by surprise, she called back, "I'm not!"

"Come on in. You can help me with sanding the spokes."

She came, red-faced, to stand just inside the door, her hands behind her back, her black eyes wary.

"Here."

He handed her a scraper used to smooth wood.

That was the beginning of Betsy's apprenticeship, which, in time, led to the first local woman to be a buggy maker. It was also the beginning of an unusual friendship between a girl and her stepfather.

He taught her many skills which proved to be exactly what she needed, her limits tested, a challenge.

When she forgot about herself and all her petty grudges, she was interesting company indeed. She told Daniel she wasn't one bit like the raven, and who did he think he was, saying that?

He threw back his head and laughed so hard she had to smile much wider than she wanted to.

"I trained that raven to eat bread. To keep you away," she said one day, when the large door was swung open and latched to the outside and the sun streamed into the dusty shop, a shaft of sunlight catching the mischief in her black eyes.

"It didn't work, did it?" he asked, grinning.

"No."

"Are you glad it didn't?"

"I'm not sure."

Daniel only smiled, kept his response to himself. She busied herself smoothing the spoke in her hand, watching his face to see why he didn't answer, then shrugged her right shoulder and ignored him. When she couldn't take the suspense, she asked, "Aren't you going to ask me what I mean?"

"What?"

"You're not listening to me."

"Yes, yes I am. But I wasn't remembering just what you said."

"I said I'm not sure if I like you or not."

"Oh. Well, I certainly hope you'll decide to like me, seeing how we have to live in the same house. And it looks as if you are going to be my right hand helper here in the shop, and it's always nice if your help likes you."

She smiled and he smiled back. And he thought how much she was like her mother, with the dark beauty in her eyes, in the contours of her cheeks, but her disposition so entirely the opposite, always rebellious, always the one who made life difficult.

Later that day, when Betsy had gone off to do other things, Paula brought out a pitcher of cold mint tea. Daniel greeted her with a smile, slipped an arm around her, and held her close.

His frau. His beloved frau.

Betsy appeared at the doorway, her breath coming in gasps.

"Dat! Mam! Come quick!"

And there he was.

Jehosophat. He sat on the lowest branch of the maple tree, preening, opening his beak to smile at them, then lowered his head and let out an awful shriek. Betsy laughed out loud, a rare sound, then threw her hands in the air.

"You old bird. You found us way down here in Robinson's Crossing."

The raven hopped off the branch and walked to them, watching warily. Paula hurried to get crusts of bread, and together they fed him the anticipated treat. Dorcas came to join them, clapping her hands in high excitement, while all around them the sun shone, the green leaves stirred in the breeze, and the scent of new wood and shavings from the shop reminded Daniel of his life's work and the blessings it had brought.

The little village surrounded them, a testimony to the willingness of a fledgling group of immigrants from Switzerland to live together in the hills of Pennsylvania, to raise children who would live there after they were gone, and their children after them. Years would go by and the buggy maker and his wife and stepdaughters would live together in happiness, the surrounding community knowing them as the wanderer who married the widow Lantz.

Gott sie gelobt und gedunkt. (God be praised and thanked.)

THE END

About the Author

LINDA BYLER WAS RAISED IN AN AMISH FAMILY and is an active member of the Amish church today. Growing up, Linda loved to read and write. In fact, she still does. Linda is well known within the Amish community as a columnist for a weekly Amish newspaper. She writes all her novels by hand in notebooks.

Linda is the author of many novels including several series, all set among the Amish communities of North America: Lizzie Searches for Love, Sadie's Montana, Lancaster Burning, Hester's Hunt for Home, The Dakota Series, The Long Road Home, and The Buggy Spoke Series for younger readers. Linda has also written a number of Christmas romances set among the Amish: *Mary's Christmas Goodbye*, *The Christmas Visitor*, *The Little Amish Matchmaker*, *Becky Meets Her Match*, *A Dog for Christmas*, *A Horse for Elsie*, and *The More the Merrier*. Linda has co-authored *Lizzie's Amish Cookbook: Favorite Recipes from Three Generations of Amish Cooks!*, *Amish Soups & Casseroles*, and *Amish Christmas Cookbook*.